DAKOTA DEATH

Cotton Lang, astride his horse, knew it could be suicide to ride across the open stretch of ground. Yet his promised bride was in great peril from the twisted love of an insane suitor. Could he yet save her? Braced against the expected volley of bullets, he spurred his mount on. Now dangerously exposed and riding low and fast, nothing less than a miracle would let him survive to even learn his sweetheart's fate.

BILLY HALL

DAKOTA DEATH

Complete and Unabridged

LINFORD
Leicester

First published in Great Britain in 2009 by
Robert Hale Limited
London

First Linford Edition
published 2009
by arrangement with
Robert Hale Limited
London

British Library CIP Data

Hall, Billy.
  Dakota death.- -(Linford western library)
  1. Western stories.
  2. Large type books.
  I. Title II. Series
  823.9'14–dc22

ISBN 978–1–84782–888–0

Published by
F. A. Thorpe (Publishing)
Anstey, Leicestershire

Set by Words & Graphics Ltd.
Anstey, Leicestershire
Printed and bound in Great Britain by
T. J. International Ltd., Padstow, Cornwall

This book is printed on acid-free paper

1

It was not a time to even think about an attempt on his life.

The March wind was raw. Cotton Lang hunched down a little deeper into his heavy coat. The collar, turned up against the wind, touched the brim of his sand-colored Stetson. Even so, the wind knifed between the two and spread its chill clear to his bones.

He shivered once, then steeled himself against the icy fingers of the north wind. He smiled in spite of his discomfort. He had come a long way from Kansas. The specters remaining from those years seldom invaded his dreams any more. Sometimes he could nearly forget the life foisted upon him during that time.

The cattle had wintered well. They would start calving in another week.

He well knew the fatigue that waited.

Calving was the best, and the worst, of life on the range. Sleep, when there was any, was snatched in no more than two-hour fragments. Sometimes cowboys would make it back to the bunkhouse for that precious couple hours. More often they would picket their horses on good grass, roll into their bedroll, and fall into the deep sleep of exhaustion.

The demands of the herd would rouse them unfailingly when they had slept a couple hours. Then they would haul still-weary bodies back into the saddle and start working through the herd. They pulled calves when necessary. They kept coyotes and wolves at bay. They did what they could to protect the newborn from weather and predators. If they did their work well and tirelessly, they would be rewarded with a good calf crop.

If their diligence lapsed, the losses could be staggering.

He was one of the lucky cowboys. He had managed to put together a small herd of his own. Isaiah Owens allowed any of his hands who wished to, to run as many as 300 head of their own stock along with his. Few cowboys took advantage of the opportunity.

Most of them, young and reckless, worked several months, collected their time, and headed for town. Once there, several months' wages disappeared quickly. Most of it ended up in the pockets of the saloon owners and the whores. When it ran out, they would pawn their saddles then their rifles then their watches or whatever else they had of value. They made the party last as long as possible.

Ranchers, on a regular basis, came to town to reclaim their hands. They paid off the things that were pawned, rehired the cowboys, and kept the ranch staffed.

The exception was round-up and calving times. During those periods any cowpoke who drew his time and left would not be welcome back. The code of the breed dictated that everyone stay on the job during what were euphemistically called 'busy times'.

Cotton had never developed a taste for liquor, and had always held the saloon whores in disdain. He lived frugally, investing his wages in cattle. He intended to own a ranch some day. He had just about enough of a herd built up to start thinking about launching out on his own. Maybe another year.

The thought instantly raised the face of Esther Owens in his mind. The daughter of his boss, she was everything he had ever dreamed of in a woman. As soon as he had the means to offer her any kind of life, he intended to ask her to be his wife.

His reverie was cut short. The angry whine of a bullet whipped past his ear. He reacted with deeply embedded instincts he hadn't used in a long time.

He left the horse's back in a long dive. Somehow he managed to whip his rifle from its scabbard even as he left the saddle.

He rolled as he hit the ground. A bullet kicked up snow and dirt just beside him. On all fours he scrambled into the edge of a shallow wash.

Hugging close to the ground, he crawled swiftly toward a lower point in the swale, coveting the greater cover. It deepened quickly into a gully, scoured out by long-past flash flood waters on their way to the South Platte River.

Leaden slugs ripped through the vegetation behind him, searching blindly for a lucky score. The smack of the rifle reports carried on the wind, always an instant later than the bullets struck.

Cotton didn't hesitate. Using the increasing depth of the gully as cover, he scrambled forward on all fours for a ways, then rose far enough to run in a crouch.

He hadn't been aware of surveying the lie of the land around himself. He simply did it by long practiced habit. He knew by the sound where the shots came from. He knew without conscious thought the route he would have to traverse to circle his attacker.

It didn't occur to him to wonder who it was.

He wasted neither time nor concentration on wondering why.

There would be time enough for that when the situation was resolved. Until then, every ounce of his concentration and action was focused on dealing with whomever had tried to kill him.

The gully he followed broadened out as it approached nearer to the river. When it did, he turned at right angles. The rise of the ground as it stretched away from the river allowed him some cover.

There was also an abundance of brush this close to a constant source of water. He scurried from plum bush to chokecherry bushes, behind tall growths of soap weeds, buck brush, wild rose thickets, and whatever cover allowed him to move unseen.

Another shallow gully opened into the broad valley of the Platte. Without hesitating, Cotton turned up the bottom of it. He slowed his pace now, watching vigilantly. Along that gully, 300 yards away, he spotted what he sought.

Stretched out in the snow, just at the rim of the gully, a man lay watching along the barrel of his rifle. Convinced he had wounded Cotton, or that he was crouched in the brush, he waited patiently. When Cotton moved, he thought he should have a clear and easy shot.

Moving silently in the snow, Cotton walked to within fifty feet of his would-be killer. He shifted his rifle to his left hand. He removed his right glove, dropping it in the snow.

'You lookin' for me?' he asked quietly.

The man on the ground stiffened as if he had been shot. Slowly he turned his head enough to see who it was behind him. He held his rifle out to one side and dropped it in the snow.

Keeping his hands well away from his body, he turned and stood up. 'How'd you get clear around behind me?' he wondered aloud.

'Rode Shanks's mares around,' Cotton

replied evenly. 'Thought I'd take a look at who's tryin' to blind side me. Who are you?'

The man shrugged. 'You don't likely know me.'

'Then why'd you try to kill me?'

'Followin' orders.'

Cotton knew the answer to the next question without asking, but asked anyway. 'Whose orders?'

'Well, that's — '

In the middle of the word, the man's hand streaked to his gun, whipping it out with the speed of a striking rattlesnake.

Cotton didn't think about his reaction. Something in his mind triggered as the man started to speak. As if moving of its own accord, his own gun appeared in his hand, spouting fire and death from its muzzle.

Two slugs slamming into his chest, one hard on the heels of the other, drove the bushwhacker backward. His unfired gun slid from his hand into the snow. He was dead even before he sprawled in the snow beside the gun that had failed him.

Cotton watched the downed gunman for several seconds. Satisfied he was dead, he walked forward. Kicking blindly through the several inches of snow, he kicked the man's gun well out of reach. He thumbed out the spent cartridges from his pistol, replaced them with fresh ones, and holstered the weapon.

He took a deep breath. 'I thought I was done with this sort of thing,' he lamented softly.

He walked back and picked up the glove he had dropped into the snow. He shook the snow off it. He slid it back onto his hand and shoved the hand inside his coat, waiting for his body heat to counter the chill of the now frigid glove.

He looked at the tracks the dead gunman had left in the snow. 'Well,' he muttered, 'let's see if we can find your horse.'

It didn't take long. It was tethered in

a thick stand of brush, easy to find only because of the tracks in the snow. He nodded when he saw the horse's brand. 'I'da bet that'd be the case,' he muttered, eyeing the Flying D brand on the horse's left hip. 'Had to be Dugger behind it.'

He led the horse back to the dead gunman. He tethered him to a scrub brush, so he could approach him from the uphill side. Even so, he grunted with the effort of hoisting the gunman's inert body across the saddle. He lashed him in place, tied the horse's reins to the saddle horn, then slapped him smartly on the rump.

His lips drawn to a thin, hard line, he watched the horse trot away. He knew he would unerringly return the gunman to Dugger's ranch. 'Guess I'm back to sleepin' with one eye open,' he acknowledged ruefully.

2

'Cotton! You could have been killed!'

Cotton nodded, smiling without mirth. 'Ain't sure why I wasn't,' he admitted. 'Guys like that don't usually miss that easy a shot. I was just ridin' along, not payin' no more attention than a greenhorn.'

Her hand on his arm communicated more than fear and concern. It radiated a warm glow that stirred the deepest parts of his being. Her eyes reflected her fear for him. 'But why would he want to kill you?'

Cotton shrugged, struggling with how much to tell her. 'Said he was just followin' orders.'

'A hired gunfighter?'

'Guess so. He said his name wouldn't mean nothin' to me. Might've been wrong about that, but hard to say. Anyway, he missed. I didn't.'

She was not distracted from the questions boiling in her mind. 'But whose orders was he following?'

'He didn't say. I asked. He acted like he was gonna tell me, but he was just usin' that to get me off guard for a second. He tried goin' for his gun instead o' answerin'.'

Her eyes bored into his intently. 'But you do have some idea who hired him, don't you?'

'Just an idea,' he hedged. 'No proof.'

'So who do you think it was? Is.'

Cotton took a deep breath. 'He was ridin' a Flyin' D horse.'

Esther Owens gasped softly. 'Dugger? He was working for Matt Dugger? You think Matt hired him to kill you.'

'Ridin' one of his horses, anyway.'

'Could he have just bought him from Matt?'

Cotton shrugged again. 'I 'spect he could've. Maybe did.'

'But you don't think so. You think Matt ordered him to kill you.'

'Seems the most likely reason he'd be

ridin' one of his horses, and lyin' out in the snow to bushwhack me.'

'Why would Matt do that? I know he doesn't like you, but why would he hire someone to kill you?'

Cotton stared deeply into the liquid pools of her dark-brown eyes. He wanted to simply dive into those eyes and never face the rest of the world again. He answered shortly, his voice harsher than he intended: 'You.'

The beauty of those incredible eyes clouded at once. 'Me? Why me?'

'You gonna tell me you don't know how much he wants you?'

Her cheeks reddened involuntarily. 'He's certainly made no secret of that,' she acknowledged. 'He's only asked me to marry him about a dozen times. Not to mention having Father suggest that to me at least as often.'

'He's got more to offer you than I do.'

'No he doesn't!'

'He's got land, lots o' cattle, good string o' horses. He could offer you a good life.'

13

Anger flashed briefly in her eyes, replaced almost at once with a very different emotion. She stepped up against him, sliding her arms around him, hugging him to herself. Head turned sideways, resting against the rough leather of his vest, she said, 'My idea of a good life would be a lifetime of being married to a man I love.'

He lowered his head so his face rested against the softness of the hair on top of her head, nestled against his chest. 'If it was him that hired the guy, he probably figures that if he gets me outa the way, you won't have a choice and you'll agree to marry him.'

'And do you think he's the only man other than you in this country that would like to marry me?'

Before he could respond, she backed away slightly. She tipped her head back, looking up into his face. An impish twist tugged at the corners of her mouth. 'And if that certain man I love doesn't get around to asking me pretty quick, I just might have to consider one of those other offers.'

He cupped her face in his deeply calloused hands. He bent forward and kissed her lightly on the lips. 'That's gonna happen just as quick as I have enough of a herd to support a family,' he asserted.

'Two can live just as cheap as one,' she shot back.

'Yeah, but I love you way too much for two to stay two for very long.'

'Oh, is that so? Here I'd just about decided you weren't all that interested in what I have to offer.'

'And just what is it you're offering?' he countered.

'Put a ring on this finger and you'll find out.'

They stood, looking into each other's eyes a long moment. The longing was equal in both faces. He took a deep breath. 'If we get a decent calf crop this spring, I'll be doin' exactly that.'

'Is that a promise?'

'That's a promise, woman of my dreams.'

'And what do you think my father will say then?'

'He'll howl and whine like a coyote with his foot in a bear trap,' Cotton admitted. As he continued, his voice took on a formal tone, as if reciting a litany he had heard enough times to mimic even the inflections of the words. 'He thinks one hundred an' fifty odd head of nondescript cattle are not nearly enough livestock to support his little girl in the manner she deserves, and to which she has become accustomed.'

'He wouldn't think twice that many was enough.' Esther snorted.

He turned serious. 'It ain't just the cattle. If there was land I could stake a claim on, then what we got now would be plenty enough for a start. Especially if we get a good calf crop. In a couple years we'll have maybe two hundred an' fifty head o' breedin' stock. But there ain't much land around here that ain't claimed.'

'Then find some somewhere else.

There's unlimited land further west.'

'I been thinkin' about that. But to do that, I'd have to go huntin' a suitable place. That'd take the whole summer, likely. It'd have to be somewhere settled enough you an' the kids'd be safe, but where there's land for the claimin', with good grass, enough hay meadows I could put up feed for winter, runnin' water year 'round. Lot to be thinkin' about.'

'Those aren't the things I've been thinking about,' she teased.

'And what sort of things might those be?'

'Wouldn't you like to know!'

'Yup. I sure would. Gonna find out, too.'

'We would be safe any place you'd build a ranch,' she asserted. 'I trust you completely. And I'm not exactly help-less either, you know. If you plan it well, we could defend the place we build against half the Sioux nation.'

'Sioux? You got a place all picked out or somethin'?'

She smiled up at him. 'Well, I have been doing some thinking. And I've talked with a lot of people, when we're in town. There's a lot of land opening up in Montana Territory. In Dakota Territory, too.'

'Lots of Indians, too.'

'But they're not like Apache or something. More like the Pawnee, and they haven't been a problem around here for a long time.'

'Lot o' difference between Sioux and Pawnee.'

They walked together, hand in hand, through the great cottonwoods along the river. He hoped she didn't notice the change in his demeanor. He had almost gotten away from long established habits of watchful alertness that had kept him alive this long. Now, with one attempt on his life, all those habits were back in full force. His eyes constantly moved, watching every shred of potential cover, every approach to their location, the top of every rise and ridge. He listened without knowing he did so, to every change of rustling leaves, every sudden flight of a bird, every noise of some animal's scurrying flight.

Even when he held her in his arms, their lips drinking deeply of each other's love, his eyes never stopped their restless sweep.

As they strolled back to the ranch yard, he hoped she wouldn't notice that he picked a route that allowed for the least opportunity for a hidden sniper.

She said nothing, but she noticed. They would have to start that life together someplace far from here, she told herself.

She had no idea how prophetic her thoughts were.

3

Cotton stepped out the front door of Aufdengarten's General Store. The single street of Ogallala's business district was almost devoid of people. Two months too early for the first trail herds of Texas cattle, activity in town was limited.

The door of Tuck's saloon slammed open against the front wall of the building. The man who burst forth onto the dirt street was average in height, but unusually broad. His neck was so thick his head almost appeared to rest on top of his shoulders. The sleeves of his flannel shirt were rolled up past the elbow. Beneath them the sleeves of his long underwear were stretched to their limit around arms more reminiscent of tree trunks than limbs. The saloon door swung shut on the tension of the springs mounted at top and bottom.

The man's head jutted forward. He leaned forward as he walked, as if to keep the head with its oversized hat from tipping him frontwards. His eyes glowered at Cotton as he charged across the street.

'Lang, I want a word with you,' he demanded.

Cotton kept all expression from his face. 'Sure you don't want to hire someone else to talk to me for you?'

Matt Dugger stopped so abruptly he nearly fell forward. 'What're you talkin' about?'

'I 'spect your horse brought the last man you hired home,' Cotton suggested quietly. 'I didn't hear about you arrangin' a public funeral for him.'

'What're you talkin' about, Lang?'

Cotton smiled tightly. 'You don't have to play dumb, Matt. Just bein' yourself is naturally dumb enough.'

Dugger's face turned deep red. His eyes deepened their baleful glare. 'I heard you been tellin' around I hired Slick Windsall to kill you,' he accused.

'As a matter of fact, I hadn't said a word about that to anybody, Matt. And I didn't even get to find out the man's name. That means the only way you could know about that is if that's exactly what you did. If you want me dead, why don't you try bein' man enough to take care of it yourself?'

'If I wanted you dead, I'd beat you to death,' Dugger declared.

'Flail away any time you think you're man enough,' Cotton invited.

Dugger lost no time accepting the challenge. With amazing quickness for such a broad, stocky man, his hamlike fist shot forward. It moved with the speed and power of a triphammer.

Knowing his opponent's temper, Cotton was already moving before the massive fist catapulted toward his face. He stepped aside, then shot a stiff right hand over the top of the young bull's arm, catching him squarely in the nose. Blood flew as if a puddle of the red fluid had been stomped on.

In the instant behind the right to the

nose, Cotton delivered a crippling left hook to the broad man's right jaw. It landed with a sickening crunch that almost certainly signaled a fractured jaw.

It failed to faze Dugger. With alarming swiftness he swung a round-house left at the side of Cotton's head. As Cotton tilted back beyond its reach, Dugger's right was already in the middle of the arc of a vicious uppercut. It was timed perfectly to coincide with Cotton's forward move, which followed his avoidance of the roundhouse left. It was aimed at nearly decapitating the smaller man.

With uncanny instincts, Cotton moved sideways at the same time he moved forward. The uppercut grazed along the left side of his face. He drove two sledge-hammer blows into Matt's midsection and dodged aside, not quite in time to avoid the heavier man's swift left hook. It caught Cotton a glancing blow on the ear. Even without absorbing the full effect of the blow, lights exploded in his head.

A ringing roar blocked out all other sound.

Instead of backing away, he responded by moving forward. Leaning forward, hunched low, almost against his antagonist, he put all of his surprising strength into three swift blows to the solar plexus. He might as well have been beating his fists against a stack of baled hay, for all the effect it had.

Matt instantly used Cotton's nearness to wrap his arms around the smaller man, seeking to catch him in a bear hug strong enough to crush his ribs.

Even as he felt the arms encircling him, Cotton straightened, driving the top of his head upward, striking the shorter man under the chin, rocking his head backward. As it recoiled forward, Cotton slammed his forehead into Matt's face. It caught him squarely in the mouth. Again, blood flew in all directions.

Unexpectedly, Cotton stomped as hard as he could on Matt's left toes, catching him totally by surprise, causing him to drop the arms that were attempting to entrap and squeeze the life from Cotton.

The instant the arms relaxed enough to release him, Cotton stepped back, then instantly forward again, driving a straight left hand to the point of Matt's chin.

Dugger could take a blow. The force of that fist against his chin would have been sufficient to stop a mad cow in her tracks. It caused the squat German to hesitate only for an instant, before he swung first his right fist, then his left, in searching arcs, seeking his opponent.

The right missed, but the left connected with Cotton's left cheekbone. It was, again, a glancing blow, but it staggered him backward.

Dugger pressed his advantage instantly, surging forward with both fists flailing away, hungrily groping for the flesh of Cotton's face.

Cotton stepped aside and circled quickly. As Dugger swiveled to face him, he sent two swift, hard jabs onto the heavy brows that jutted over his eyes. Both blows opened deep gashes that instantly caused blood to flow downward into his eyes.

Cursing fiercely, Dugger swiped at the blood, trying to clear his vision. Cotton began a steady barrage of quick blows, moving back and forth in front of, and to the sides of the stronger man. His iron hard fists quickly made mincemeat of the man's face, reducing it to a ragged and bleeding mass.

Abruptly the rain of blows stopped. Cotton stepped back, then forward, putting every ounce of weight and muscle into a straight right hand. It landed with the sound of a sledgehammer on a wooden post.

For a moment, Dugger stood perfectly still. Then he toppled forward, unconscious, into the dirt of Ogallala's street.

Cotton reached down and grabbed him by the hair. He turned his head sideways to allow the unconscious man to breath, and walked away.

Reaching a water trough, he sloshed water onto his face and washed his hands. He was surprised to see the water in the trough turn red. 'Must've caught me more times than I realized,' he muttered. 'Sure got my ears ringin', anyway.'

A voice from the board sidewalk surprised him. 'You should've kilt him while you had the chance.'

He wiped the water from his face and eyed the speaker. He was a thin whip of a man, maybe fifty years old. He wore a well-used Colt revolver tied low on his right hip. *Tougher'n whang leather*, popped into Cotton's head as he studied the old cowpoke.

'Think so?' he asked noncommitally.

The old man bobbed his head. 'You're gonna have to, sooner or later.'

'Why do you say that?'

The old man grinned suddenly. 'Well, everybody in the country knows he's sweet on your girl. He'll either kill you to have her, or you'll have to kill him.'

'You seem to know a lot about what goes on,' Cotton observed. 'Who're you?'

'Name's Cap Lindiken. I work for the Lonergan brothers.'

'The Rafter L L,' Cotton said.

'Yeah, that and the Deuce L and the Rafter L Bar.'

'I'd noticed they used some different brands.'

'They're bringin' in some blooded stock. Keep the different herds separate thataway. They don't leave much land for a young fella to start up on, though. I'm sure that's crossed your mind more'n once.'

Cotton had the uneasy feeling the man was reading his mind. 'What makes you think that matters to me?'

Cap chuckled. 'You don't think folk've noticed you buildin' up a herd o' your own? A man thinkin' about havin' a family and a place of his own's gotta be thinking about land.'

Cotton turned to one side. Holding one side of his nose shut with a finger, he blew the blood out of one nostril. He repeated the action with the other nostril, clearing it so he could breathe. He turned back to Lindiken. 'You size things up pretty well for someone I don't even know. Is there a reason you're telling me all this?'

Cap grinned. 'I don't do much without a reason,' he affirmed. 'Like to stay ahead o' the game. I'm guessin' you'll be takin' your herd and headin' for greener pastures one o' these days. I'm sorta beginnin' to feel closed in, around here. Too many people settlin' in this country. Then there's all them Texas trail herds comin' in every summer. I need some open space. I just wanted to put in a word to trail along whenever you head out. You'll be needin' some hands you can trust. Not just for the trail, but after you get where you're headin'.'

Cotton tenderly probed his fingers around the places on his face that were already beginning to swell. 'Have you trailed some herds before?'

'I've trailed with half a dozen. Been the trail boss with four. Brought some herds o' Chisholm's up. Couple o' McIntyre's. Some to Kansas. Couple here after the railroad got this far.'

'That's a lot o' time on the trail.'

'Too much,' Cap admitted. 'Makes an old man out've a fella. Keepin' some o' them Texas cowboys in line is like tryin' to keep a bunch o' bobcats corralled in a cactus patch.'

'But you're puttin' in for another trail job anyway,' Cotton observed.

'I guess I'm a bear for punishment,' Cap grinned. Then he got serious again. 'You ain't got that big of a herd, though, and you won't have a bunch o' Texas rowdies to deal with. I got close to a hundred head o' my own cows I'd be wantin' to bring along, too.'

Cotton nodded. 'I'll keep it in mind,' he promised.

'You might best keep that fella you whipped in mind right now,' Cap suggested. He jutted his chin toward Matt Dugger, who was beginning to stir. 'I don't think he's ever been whipped in a stand-up fight afore. Ain't no tellin' how he's gonna take it.'

Cotton nodded, watching the defeated rancher carefully. He strolled over and picked his hat out of the dirt, knocked the dust off it, and clapped it on his head. Then he walked over and pulled Dugger's forty-five from its holster. He thumbed the shells out of it, letting them fall into the street. Then he jammed it back in the rancher's holster.

He knelt down on one knee, grabbed Dugger by the hair and lifted his head. When the downed man's eyes eventually focused on his face, he spoke. 'Listen, Dugger, and listen good. Esther Owens is my woman. Now, and for keeps. You butt out an' stay out. If you don't leave her alone, I'll kill you like a mangy coyote. Don't you forget.'

He let loose of Dugger's hair abruptly. The rancher's face nearly plowed into the dirt before he was able to arrest its descent.

Cotton watched for a moment, as the

blood dripped steadily from Dugger's face, making a dark puddle in the street. Then he strode to his horse and stepped into the saddle. With a curt nod to Cap Lindiken, he trotted toward the livery barn at the far end of Ogallala's main street.

4

'Got a minute, Cotton?'

Alarms sounded in the back of Cotton's mind. His hand automatically dropped within inches of his gun butt. He turned to the voice that addressed him, and relaxed. 'Mornin', Chet,' he greeted. 'You're in town early.'

Chet Holland rolled the match in his mouth over to one corner. 'Mite jumpy, are you? I thought you was gonna slap leather on me for a second there.'

'Sorry,' Cotton apologized. 'Got shot at the other day. Tends to make a man jittery.'

'That so? Who shot at ya?'

Cotton shrugged. 'He didn't offer his name. He did think he'd make a second try instead. He wasn't fast or smart either one.'

'You don't say! You know why he was after you?'

'Said he'd been paid to get rid of me.'

Chet's eyebrows rose. 'And I'm bettin' you got a good idea who was doin' the payin',' he observed.

'Didn't take a lot o' figurin',' Cotton admitted. 'He seemed to know the man's name, anyway. We had a couple words about it.'

Chet grinned. 'So that's what that was about. I heard you beat the snot outa Matt Dugger. From what I hear, it's the first time anyone ever so much as laid a hand on him in a stand-up fight.'

'He's a tough boy, all right. Workin' on his gut is like poundin' on a tree-trunk. I don't think I've ever seen anyone as stout as he is.'

Chet nodded. 'I seen him pick up a spring wagon all by himself once. He bet Norman Underwood a twenty-dollar gold piece he could do it. Got underneath with his back against the bed of it, then straightened out his legs. Lifted all four wheels clean off the ground.'

'That's a lot of lift,' Cotton admired.

Chet grinned. 'More'n he bargained for. He went an' locked his knees when he got 'em straight. Then he couldn't unlock 'em to put 'er down. Four guys had to lift most of the weight off of him so he could set it back down.'

Cotton grinned in response. 'Did he get his twenty bucks?'

'He collected it. Norman put up a little bit of an argument, but he hadn't stipulated that Dugger had to set it back down again by himself. He sure enough lifted it. I ain't sure whether he agreed or didn't wanta have to challenge Dugger to keep from payin' up.'

'Dugger ain't someone most folks wanta tangle with,' Cotton agreed.

'What's your plans?' Chet asked, changing the subject abruptly.

'Plans for what?'

'Well, you ain't gettin' any younger,' Chet observed. 'You got a pretty good starter herd built up, but no place at all to run 'em on, if you quit Owens. There's not all that much land left unclaimed around here. Unless you rob a bank to get money to buy someone out, your options would seem to be a little bit limited.'

Cotton studied the rancher carefully. 'What are you drivin' at, Chet?'

'Well, I'm fixin' to throw a proposition at ya,' Chet announced. 'I went and sold out.'

Cotton nodded, showing no surprise. 'I've heard rumors you sold your place.'

'Lock, stock and barrel,' Chet confirmed. Then he quickly qualified it. 'Well, not the stock. Just the lock and barrel, I guess. I sold the land and buildings.'

'Who to?'

'Lonergans.'

'That's what I'd heard, all right. Word gets around, in this country. Well, it figures. They're workin' on ownin' half the country, it looks like.'

'Sign of the times,' Chet confirmed. 'The big guys get bigger, and us little guys get out or get run over or swallowed up.'

'You ain't exactly a little guy,' Cotton argued. 'You must have upwards of a thousand head o' cattle.'

Chet nodded. 'I got a good herd built up. It'll run to upwards of twelve hundred head.'

'And you didn't sell 'em to Lonergans. What are you plannin' to do with 'em?'

'That's what I wanted to talk to you about. Got some time?'

'Sure. How about we swing over to the Ogallala House and work on a cup o' their coffee while we gab.'

'Sounds good. They got good coffee.'

'Good food, too.'

'Best around,' Chet agreed.

Ten minutes later they were seated at a round table in the dining room of the Ogallala House hotel and restaurant. The large window before them offered a clear view of most of Ogallala's main street.

'You've trailed with some herds, ain't ya, Cotton?' Chet asked.

Cotton nodded. 'Some.'

'You were the trail boss on a couple drives, I've heard.'

Cotton nodded. 'Three.'

'How big o' herds?'

'One was upwards o' three thousand head. Others were about half that.'

'How much did you lose?'

'Less'n one per cent.'

Chet whistled. 'That's impressive. The normal amount is closer to ten per cent, ain't it?'

Cotton nodded. 'It depends. A lot depends on weather, what bunch of Indians are doin' what, who you got for hands, how far you're trailin' 'em. There's a lot o' things that figure in.'

'Even so, one per cent loss, on three different drives, is about as good a numbers as I've heard. Why'd you quit?'

'Dead-end life,' Cotton replied. 'Pretty good money, but no chance to do much with it.'

'More to it than that, I'm guessin'.'

Cotton hesitated only a moment. 'Well, when I was here with the last herd I ramrodded, I met Esther Owens. I decided it was time to think about settlin' down.'

'So now what you need the most is a place to settle on.'

'That's about the size of it.'

Chet leaned back and shoved his hat to the back of his head. 'Up in Montana Territory there's a lot of land that's finer than any land you've ever seen. There for the claimin'. Just enough people fillin' in to have a town here an' there, especially over east, toward Dakota Territory. Enough to have supplies available, even a school and a church maybe. Not like plumb wilderness, but not overrun with people like it's gettin' to be around here.'

Cotton felt his pulse accelerate. He sat up a bit straighter. 'You been up there?'

Chet nodded. 'Twice. Just lookin' around. I want more land than what's available around here. I like country that ain't quite so settled, too. I got my eye on a patch o' ground up there that'll run upwards o' ten thousand head. Good runnin' water. Fine grass. Hay meadows five miles long. Shelter a-plenty for stormy times. Room for my boys to have a spread of their own when they get old enough. Far enough from a town to not be crowded. Close enough to get there in a day for supplies.'

'How old are the boys? You got three of 'em, right?'

Chet nodded. 'Three o' the finest boys you'll ever set eyes on. Johnny's twelve. Ezekiel's ten. Sam's seven, an' danged near man enough to whip either one o' the older ones.'

Cotton grinned. 'I saw him during brandin' over at your place last year. His horse started buckin' on 'im. Rode 'im like he'd been doin' it twenty years.'

Chet chuckled. 'Little rascal thinks he can do anything anyone else has ever done. If he lives to grow up, he's gonna be a handful.'

'What does your wife think of the idea?'

'Oh, she's all for it. She's as restless a

spirit as I am. I got three married hands, too, so it ain't like she'd be the only woman in the outfit.' He leaned forward toward Cotton, looking for all the world like a snake-oil salesman seeking to close a big deal. 'That's why I thought of you. There's enough other women in the country that the women goin' up with us won't feel isolated. And there's another spot, less'n ten miles east of the one I got my eye on, that'd make a fine ranch for a guy startin' out. There's a pretty decent little town less than thirty miles away. It'd make a fine place for you and Esther to slap a claim on.'

Cotton worked to disguise how madly his mind was racing with the possibilities. 'Your hands are stickin' with you?'

'All but a couple. I got five hands that're plumb gung-ho to head north. Two of the neighbors want to go too. What we need is a trail boss. That's what I wanted to talk to you about.'

'How you plannin' to get there?'

41

Chet took a long breath. 'I figure we can skirt the west end of the sand hills, push up through the pine ridge country in northern Nebraska, stay betwixt the badlands and the Black Hills, then angle west a ways when we get past the Black Hills. The land I got my eye on stretches from the Pumpkin to the Tongue rivers. No mountains to cross. No big rivers. It oughta be doable.'

'You know Cap Lindiken?' Cotton asked abruptly.

'Sure. I've known Cap a long while. Why?'

'What do you know about him?'

Chet studied Cotton carefully. 'Well, I know he's as honest as the day is long. He's hell on high red wheels in a fight. He can shoot the eye out of a sparrow at a hundred yards. Don't know how he came to end up in this country, but I've never heard anything but good about him. Why?'

'He's feelin' pretty cramped around here too,' Cotton explained. 'He talked to me on the street yesterday. He seems to think the same as you do, that I'm about due to be looking for a chunk of land somewhere. He asked to trail along whenever I do. He's got about a hundred head of his own stuff.'

'You don't say!'

'He might make you a good trail boss.'

Chet studied Cotton closely. 'Are you sayin' you ain't interested?'

'Just wonderin' why you're askin' me instead of him.'

Relief flooded Chet's face. 'Just because you're a good twenty years younger. Cap's old enough some o' the guys might think they've gotta challenge him once in a while. Especially when the word gets around about what you did to Dugger, not to mention the hired gun that tried to kill you, nobody's gonna be nearly as apt to call your hand. That stops most squabblin' amongst the crew afore it ever gets started.'

'What if I wanted to hire Cap as straw boss?'

'Now that'd make us the finest trail crew any man ever dreamed of. You an' Cap both? Along with the rest of my hands? And we'll need to hire at least half a dozen more. It don't get no better'n that! Are you sayin' you'll do it?'

Cotton took a deep breath. 'I'm sure enough inclined to. I'll be wantin' to talk to Esther. This is a bunch to think about. How soon do you need an answer?'

'Oh, yesterday would probably be soon enough.'

Cotton chuckled. 'How about a couple or three days from now?'

'Take your time, just so you hurry up while you're doin' it,' Chet assured him. 'We can't head north until we're done calvin' and the calves is old enough to travel. Even then, it'll be slow trailin'.'

Cotton nodded. 'It'll be a whole lot different than pushin' a bunch o' steers to market, that's for sure. Cows an' calves won't cover a whole lot o' ground for the first month or so.'

'We'll be doin' good to get there and settled in afore winter weather hits,' Chet agreed.

Cotton's churning stomach told him a lot of surprises would unfold between now and then.

5

'I was under the distinct impression you were ordered to stay away from me and leave me alone.'

Esther Owens' eyes flashed fire. Her stance belied the deep fear that churned in her stomach.

Matt Dugger had caught her well away from the house. She had been searching for early spears of asparagus that grew wild along the river. The large pile of the succulent spears cradled in her apron served as her only barrier, keeping the burly rancher at least that far away.

Dugger's own eyes flashed dangerously through the darkly discolored, puffy swelling that surrounded them. His nose was still swollen to nearly twice its normal size. Bruises and lacerations covered almost every patch of skin on his inflated visage. Esther resisted the urge to comment on the job Cotton had done on the big man's face.

He winced at her words. 'Ain't nobody tells me who I can talk to and who I can't,' he growled.

'I doubt you'd be willing to say that to Cotton,' she shot back.

The red hue of his battered face deepened. His head thrust forward another notch. For just an instant, something in his eyes looked less than rational. The look was gone as quickly as it had appeared. 'You'd just as well forget about that windbag,' he asserted.

Her eyebrows rose. 'Oh? And why would I do that?'

'Just because his chances o' comin' back from that lame-brained cattle drive are somewhere betwixt slim an' none,' Dugger declared.

'He is very capable of taking care of himself,' she argued. Then she couldn't resist the urge to add, 'You should be very well aware of that fact.'

Dugger, uncharacteristically, ignored the jibe. 'Not where he's a-headin',' he fired back. 'He's bitin' off a heap more'n he can chew, this time.'

'What makes you so sure of that?'

'It just stands to reason,' he hedged. 'Too many things stacked against 'im. If the Indians don't wipe 'em out the weather and the rattlesnakes will. There ain't no way they can drive that many cattle five hundred or more miles through that country, and get there alive.'

'He's done it before,' she asserted. 'He's brought several trail herds up from Texas, and lost fewer cattle than anyone else ever claimed to.'

'It's a whole lot different drivin' 'em from Texas to here, than it is headin' north into Indian country, where there ain't been no herds taken before.'

'He's capable of it. He can do just about anything he sets his mind to.'

'Yeah, includin' findin' what he's lookin' for out there an' not comin' back.'

Her face flared red. 'He's found exactly what he wants already,' she declared hotly.

Dugger snorted. 'If he'd found what he wanted, he'd have claimed you already, instead o' headin' outa the country without you.'

'He's doing exactly as we planned,' she stated.

He snorted again. 'Exactly as he planned,' he argued. 'If he was really aimin' to marry you, he'd do it, and take you along, like the other married guys is doin'. I bet he ain't even mentioned that, has he?'

'As a matter of fact he has,' she contradicted. 'We have discussed that fully. When he has a place for a ranch established, he'll come back and we'll be married then. He doesn't want me to have to live out of a covered wagon while he builds a house and everything.'

Dugger turned his best condescending look on her. 'And you actually believe that, do you? Why, I'll bet you don't even know a stinkin' thing about him, afore he showed up in this country.'

Her lips drew down to a thin, straight

line. 'I have neither need nor desire to discuss my fiancé with you, Matt Dugger. Nor do I have any desire to continue this conversation with you. Please go away and leave me alone. I do not wish to speak to you again.'

He opened his mouth twice and closed it silently again. The wild, irrational look crossed his eyes again, then left as swiftly as it had come. At last he said, changing the belligerence of his tone to one of earnest pleading. 'Aw, now, Esther, don't go bein' that way. I come here to offer to marry you.'

She raised up to the full height of her five foot three inches. 'You came here to offer to marry me? To offer? You came here to make such a generous, wonderful offer, as if it were something grand you were offering? As if I were a desperately ugly old spinster with no hopes of matrimony unless some noble, self-sacrificing saint offered to rescue me from spinsterhood. You came here to offer?'

'Aw, now, I didn't mean it thataway,'

he protested, sputtering. His confusion at her anger was evident. 'I meant I come to ask you. To ask you if you'd marry me. I already talked to your pa. He agrees with me a hundred per cent. I can offer you a good life. I got the means to give you security. You know all about me. Not like that gunfighter that's likely got warrants out for him in half a dozen places. You could do lots worse than marryin' me.'

She stomped a foot and glared daggers at him. 'Right now I can't think of anything in the world that would be any worse than being desperate enough to marry you. Now go away! Leave me alone!'

'I don't aim to leave you alone,' he differed. 'I want you to marry me.'

The wild look in his eyes returned. It sent shivers down her spine, but she was determined not to let it show. 'If you don't leave this place right now, I will tell Cotton that you have defied his warning and approached me. If I do that, he will kill you as surely as if you

51

were a rattlesnake in the outhouse. Which is not a bad analogy, by the way.'

His face turned bright red. His eyes bulged. She thought for a moment he might either have a fit of apoplexy or lose all self-control entirely. He sputtered, trying to find words adequate to express his anger that would be fit for her ears. At last he fumed, 'It'll be a cold day in hell when I let that Texas windbag tell me anything. You just wait, Esther Owens. He ain't gonna be around long anyhow. Chet Holland thinks he's the best trail boss in the country for his stinkin' cattle drive. What he don't know is that when that Texas drifter pulls out with 'em, we've done seen the last o' him. He ain't comin' back from that cattle drive. Not unless they haul him back, all laid out in the back of a wagon. You ain't never gonna see that troublemaker alive again, I'm tellin' you. And when he's dead and cold, we'll see how uppity you are. You'll be beggin' me to marry you then.'

That icy wind swept up her spine again. His words felt like an icicle stabbing through her heart. He said Cotton was not going to return with absolute certainty. She fought to keep her voice even as she answered, 'And just what makes you so sure he won't survive the cattle drive?'

Dugger blinked several times, knowing he'd already said more than he should have. His eyes lost the strange look. 'I know things,' he evaded. 'I'm tellin' you, he ain't comin' back. And I'll be here to watch you talkin' out of the other side of your mouth then, you high an' mighty little hussy.'

He wheeled and stalked to his horse. He hauled himself into the saddle. Jerking the horse's head around savagely with the reins, he clamped the spurs to his side. Esther stood watching him until he disappeared through the trees that flanked the river.

She took a deep, ragged breath. She hadn't realized how terrified she had been, to have been caught so far away from the house, alone, by Matt Dugger. Now that he was gone, she wasn't sure her trembling legs were going to hold her up.

The realization struck her that Dugger had known exactly where she was. Her eyes flashed fire. Her jaw clamped into a hard line, a small bunch of muscle knotting at the jaw's hinge. Her lips pursed tightly together.

She was still walking in long, angry strides as she entered the Double O Bar ranch yard. She spotted her father by the corrals, and marched directly to him. As she strode to within a yard of him, she abruptly dropped the apronful of asparagus. She stabbed an angry finger at him. Her voice was brittle with her fury. 'You told him where I was!' she accused.

Her father backed up a step. The two cowhands he was talking with looked at one another. As one, they beat a hasty retreat, heading anywhere away from the ferocity of her anger.

'What are you talking about?' Ike

Owens protested.

'You know very well what I'm talking about, Father,' she accused again. 'You told Matt Dugger where I was.'

Ike looked like he would rather be facing a cougar in a corner than standing where he was. 'Well . . . well, why wouldn't I? His intentions are honorable. You don't have to be afraid of him.'

'That man has never had an honorable intention in his whole life,' she differed. 'I don't know why you even want to be friends with him, and I will never, ever consider marriage to him, even if it means I die an old maid.'

'Now, Esther,' he protested, 'you could do lots worse than Matt. He ain't no handsome and dashing knight in shining armor or nothin', but he's steady. He's got a good spread.'

'He's got a ranch he has stocked with stolen cattle and a crew of hardcase criminals,' she challenged. 'He is the one man in this country that I am just flat out afraid of. And you told him exactly where I was. Alone. Clear out of

55

earshot of the yard, even. How could you possibly, ever, do that to me?'

'Now I don't see how you can be afraid of Matt. If you're afraid of anyone, it oughta be that gunslinger you're so sweet on. Who knows what all he's done, back in Kansas or wherever it is he's runnin' from?'

'He is not running from anything,' she yelled. 'And it is my business who I choose to spend my life with. And I want to know what Matt Dugger meant when he said he was sure Cotton wouldn't be coming back from the cattle drive unless he was hauled back in a wagon, dead. Do you know anything about that?'

Ike's attitude changed abruptly. 'He said that?'

'Yes, he said that! He said the only way Cotton was going to come back, is cold and dead in the bed of a wagon. He said when that happens, I'll be happy enough to marry him then. Do you have something to do with whatever he has planned?'

Ike shook his head. 'I don't know nothin' about no plans. You oughta know me better'n that. I ain't got no idea what he meant. I 'spect he just meant there's a lot o' peril where he'll be headin' with that herd. Most anything could happen. He's prob'ly right in figgerin' the chances ain't very good that he'll make it all the way there and back again.'

She stamped her foot, smashing several pieces of the carefully gathered asparagus. 'He will make it back,' she declared, putting strong emphasis on the 'will.' Without taking a breath she continued, 'And when Cotton comes back I will marry him, whether you like it or not. And if you ever put me in a spot like that with Matt Dugger again, I will saddle up my horse and ride after Cotton, wherever he goes, and you will never see me again for the rest of your life!'

Every time she said the word 'will,' her voice rose several decibels, emphasizing the word with increasingly hot intensity.

'You don't mean that, Esther. You're just mad, right now.'

'You bet your life I'm mad right now,' she screamed at him. 'And the more I talk to you the madder I'm getting. Go . . . go . . . find a cow to chase or something.'

She turned her back on him and began to scoop up the scattered asparagus sprouts from the ground. Ike beat a hasty retreat, hoping his daughter would cool off before supper time.

6

'Howdy, Alf.'

Alfred Fankhouser nodded affably to Cotton. 'Mornin', Cotton. Gettin' about set to head north?'

'Gettin' close,' Cotton acknowledged. 'Brandin' went well. Wagons are lined up. Just about got enough hands hired on to handle things.'

'Gonna be a long trail.'

'Yup. It sure is. Even if everything goes just right, it'll be a long trail.'

'And things don't never go just right.'

Cotton chuckled appreciatively. 'I ain't seen it happen yet, anyway.'

'I hear you're goin' with mules.'

Cotton nodded. 'We've put together two teams of mules for each of the wagons, with a dozen extra mules to spell any that come up lame. We got some really big mules.'

'Well, they'll outlast horses, that's for

'sure,' Alfred approved. 'Not near as slow as oxen.'

Cotton signified his agreement. 'Oxen might be fast enough,' he mused, 'seein' as how we gotta go slow enough for all the cows an' calves to keep up. But the mules can run flat out for a ways if we get in a spot where they need to.'

'You figure you might need to?'

Cotton shrugged. 'You never know. Lot o' country 'twixt here an' there.'

'Lot o' Indians, you mean.'

'Indians,' Cotton agreed, 'as well as a lot of other people. There's some bad apples makin' a livin' off the hard work of others out there.'

'So what can I do for you?' Alfred asked abruptly. 'You lookin' to hire some o' my hands out from under me?'

Cotton hesitated just briefly. 'Well, just one in particular. Rusty came and talked to me yesterday. He wants to hire on for the trip.'

'Rusty!'

'Yup. I told him I'd ask you. He wasn't any too happy about me talkin' to you afore I gave him an answer, but I thought it was only right.'

Alfred's eyes were wide with disbelief. 'He's only fifteen!'

Cotton nodded. 'I know it. Big for his age, though. Good hand with horses or cows either one. He just about don't miss with a rope. Tougher'n whang leather, that kid is.'

'But he's only fifteen!'

'How old were you when you first hired out as a cowpoke?'

Alfred hesitated a long moment. 'I was thirteen. But that was different. Times was different then.'

'Yeah, but kids ain't. He's plumb anxious to try his wings.'

'Cotton, you're headin' into country that's still plumb wild. There's three or four different tribes of Indians between here and there. There's likely a passel o' thunderstorms and cyclones and God knows what all else that can stampede a herd. Seasoned men get killed doin' what you're askin' me to let my kid do.'

'I'm not askin' you to, Alf. I'm just

doin' what I told Rusty I'd do. He asked to sign on. I told him I wouldn't take him without your say-so.'

Alfred Fankhouser was silent for several minutes. Cotton did not interrupt the rancher's thoughts. At last he said, 'His ma'll raise the devil with me if I let him go. But if I don't let him go on this one, there'll be another one come along. He won't likely ask next time. He's headstrong, that boy is. Gets it, along with that red hair, from his ma.'

'Couldn't have gotten any of it from you,' Cotton suggested, tongue in cheek.

Alfred smiled briefly, then grew somber again. 'The first time I let him ride a bronc, his ma just about came unglued. He was twelve, but he could stick to a saddle like a cockleburr to a wool blanket. Rode him just fine. But I'd just as well have been sleepin' in the barn for the next month.'

Cotton smiled sympathetically. 'Mothers tend to be pretty protective.'

Alfred took a deep, ragged breath.

His eyes were pleading as he looked at Cotton. 'You'll take good care of the boy? His ma'll die if anything happens to him.'

'I'll do my best,' Cotton replied. 'I can't promise you that nothin'll happen to him, though. You know that.'

'Yeah, I know. But it'll ease my mind some to know you're at least tryin' to look out for him.'

'I'll do what I can.'

Alfred studied the ground for a moment. 'I suppose it'd be sorta cowardly to let him be the one to tell his ma what he's gonna do.'

'I sure ain't gonna tell you how to handle that,' Cotton asserted quickly.

'You just wait,' Alfred predicted. 'You'll find out what this is like. You gonna marry Esther and take her along?'

Cotton shook his head. 'I'll find a spot for a ranch first. Then I'll come back for her. Thirsty Williams is gonna keep his eyes open, kinda look after 'er for me. He'll see she's safe and sound till I get back.'

'She'll wait for you,' Alfred said with conviction.

Cotton did not answer, letting the rancher wrestle with his thoughts.

'It's not fair, you know,' he said after a bit.

'What's not fair?'

'Life. Kids. Raisin' a family.'

'What do you mean?'

'Well, it's just like with Rusty. We spent some of the hardest years of our life, raising him this far. We nursed him when he was sick. We taught him to walk and talk. I showed him how to handle a rope and a gun. I let him get banged up good now and then, learnin' how to handle a horse. Together, we taught him all the things we could teach him about life. And slowly, bit by bit, day by day, he grew up. He changed. He learned. He came to a point where he was just a plumb delight to be around, and a fine hand to work with.'

'He's a fine boy.'

'Yes, he is. And now that we've done our job well, it's time for him to leave.'

'That's the way of life.'

'I know it is. That's exactly what I meant. It ain't fair.'

'It's not like you're losing him.'

'Sure it is,' Alfred disagreed flatly. 'That's just exactly what it's like. That's what it is. He's leaving. He's setting out on his own. Spreading his wings. I know that's the way it's supposed to be, and he's all happy and excited about it. He don't hardly give a thought to the hole he's leaving in this house when he leaves.'

'But he'll be back.'

'Maybe. Someday. Then again, maybe we'll never see him again. We may never even know what happens to him. Or maybe he will come back again before we're dead, but he won't be the same. By that time he'll have finished growing up. All the boy will be gone out of his face. His shoulders and chest will be all filled out. His eyes will be different, because he'll have learned his share of pain. Some of the dance will be gone outa those eyes, and there'll be a lot more depth there. No, he won't be the same at all. He'll be all changed. But I won't have gotten to watch the change, and it won't really be like my boy come back at all. It'll be a man come back, that used to be my boy. But then, just like now, he won't need me.'

'But he'll still love you.'

'Oh, I'm sure he will. And I'll still love him. But he won't need me. That's the way I know we did a good job raising him. He doesn't need us now. If you do a good job as a parent, the kid grows to where he doesn't need you any more, and then he's gone. It just doesn't seem fair.'

'It hurts, doesn't it?'

'Yeah. Yeah, it hurts. But I gotta let 'im go. Just try to look after him some for me.'

Cotton couldn't help but feel the rancher's hurt as he rode slowly back to the Double O Bar. The thought of being personally responsible for the youngster's safety rode heavier on him than anything he could remember.

7

Branding time had already faded to a cherished memory. It had been a good year for the cattle. A mild winter cost few casualties among the herd. An abundant crop of healthy calves cavorted and played as their mothers fattened on the rich grass.

'Providential,' Cotton mused, 'that cows are actually gainin' fat while they got calves suckin'. Sure gonna make a lot easier drive north.'

The herd was assembled well north of the Platte River, swollen as it was with the run-off from snow melt and spring rains. Each of the five families among the group was outfitted with a covered wagon that would be home for the next several months. In addition, seven wagons of supplies were loaded and ready to roll, each pulled by a large team of mules. After a lot of discussion they had added another dozen teams of mules, to allow each team to rest every other day. Cotton had sent Cap and another hand nearly to Iowa, buying mules.

Their return with the mules brought an additional surprise.

'What's the wagon?' Cotton queried.

Cap grinned. 'Ace in the hole. Somethin' I thought we just might need. Ain't gonna tell you no more, less'n we need it.'

Anger welled up instantly in Cotton. He fought to stifle it. He was trail boss of this endeavor. He had a right to know what everyone was bringing along.

As soon as the thought reared itself in his mind, another countered it. He didn't, in fact, know what hardly any of the others had packed away in their wagons. He knew it was customary to have wagons built with cleverly concealed false bottoms for valuables and precious keepsakes. Even in the rest of the wagons, he had only minimal knowledge of the contents.

Instead of demanding to know what Cap had procured, he asked instead, 'Who's the driver?'

'Name's Tuffy Winthrop. Everyone just calls him 'Sarge'. He's an old friend of mine.'

'I've run into him,' Cotton replied. 'I thought he was in the army, stationed at Fort Kearny.'

'He was,' Cap confirmed. 'His hitch is up. He thought he'd like to toss in with us, 'stead o' re-uppin', see a little new country. As long as you don't mind, o' course.'

Several thoughts ran through Cotton's mind, but he swiftly dismissed them. He trusted Cap. He had to. Cap was his second in command. He had right to give a friend permission to accompany the group. He would obviously be in charge of whatever Cap had procured for the trip.

He changed the course of the conversation abruptly. 'You find enough good mules?'

Cap nodded with enthusiasm. 'Not just good ones. We come up with the best bunch o' mules I ever seen in my life. They got size and strength, and gentle as they come. They're good enough you may end up ridin' mules afore we're through.'

Cotton chuckled. 'Don't hold your breath. Mules are good for pullin', but I ain't about to ride one.'

Cap gave voice to a random thought the conversation had triggered. 'I seen a fella ride a buffalo once,' he said.

'A buffalo?'

'Yup. Saddle and all. Had to more'n double the length of the cinch. Pertneart needed a ladder to climb onto it. Him and that saddle looked plumb ridiculous on top of that critter, but he had it well trained. Rode it everywhere.'

'What for?'

Cap shrugged. 'Just cuz he could, I guess. Raised it from a calf. Plumb gentle.'

'I bet he scared the liver out've every horse he got close to.'

Cap chuckled. 'Yeah, he did that. Folks sure hated seein' him come to town. Pertneart caused a stampede every time.'

Cotton brought the conversation back from its digression. 'We plan on pullin' out day after tomorrow. Cookie'll leave with the chuck wagon tomorrow, and have things set up for first camp.'

'How far we goin' the first day?'

'Just to Ash Hollow. Little less than five miles.'

Cap nodded. ''Bout right. Give us time to get 'em used to the idea of trailin'.'

Cotton nodded his agreement. 'I'd like to make ten miles a day after they get used to it,' he offered. 'That'll get us there in good time to get everything settled in before winter. It'll take a week or two to work up to that, though.'

His estimate proved accurate. Five miles was a superb achievement the first day. Not used to the idea of being driven, the cattle were particularly reluctant to keep moving. A total of eighteen men were in the saddle. Women drove all but one of the six covered wagons. Eight supply wagons, and the mysterious wagon driven by Sarge Winthrop, added up to a total of fifteen wagons, twenty-seven men, seven women and nine children, ranging from infants to nearly grown. It took all the skill and effort of every man in the saddle to keep the herd together, and to keep it moving.

★ ★ ★

A broad meadow with a clear stream running through it provided welcome rest for men and animals. Camp had been set up at the upstream end of the meadow, suddenly filled with more than 1,500 cattle. The wranglers kept the remuda of combined horses and mules separate from the cattle, but within easy access of good grass and water.

'Gonna leave a trail of eaten-down and trampled grass for six hundred miles,' Cotton mused. 'Anybody lookin' for us sure ain't gonna have any trouble findin' our trail.'

The words were no sooner out of his mouth than chips flew from a tree trunk inches from his horse's head. It was followed an instant later by the report of a rifle. The animal squealed in pain and surprise as the splinters sprayed his face. He plunged way, pitching and dancing.

The animal's reaction probably saved Cotton from the hidden rifle's second shot. It whined past his ear, inducing his dive from the saddle into the cover of a plum bush.

Cursing silently as the thorny branches of the plum bush raked at his skin, he scurried behind the trunk of a fallen tree. Bark flew from it, inches from his head, even as he ran.

He crawled to the branched end of the downed tree, finding a spot that allowed him to survey the hill from which the shots emanated. Removing his hat, he peered between branches.

Instantly a bullet shattered the

branch an inch above his head, showering him once again with bark and debris.

Ducking back down, Cotton surveyed his situation. He had his rifle. Somehow, by virtue of long practice, he had jerked it from its scabbard as he dived from the saddle. But there was no other adequate cover anywhere close. There were some trees, but neither large nor dense enough to provide an escape route. The thin brush was no barrier to a well-placed bullet. From where his assailant was ensconced, he had a clear view of every inch of ground for at least a hundred yards in all directions. He was enough higher than Cotton's position that the tall grass afforded no concealment whatever.

'Can't even stick my head up long enough to figure out where he's at,' Cotton fumed.

He crawled back to the base of the uprooted tree, where its torn roots thrust twisted spears and tendrils upward. Dirt clung stubbornly to them, as if reluctant to let them escape. As he sought a spot that would afford him a concealed view of the hillside, another bullet ripped past his face.

Hugging the ground, he retreated to the safety of the tree's main trunk. 'Pinned down tighter'n the skin on a bedbug,' he gritted.

He glanced at the sky. It still lacked an hour until dark. Unfortunately, a full moon had already risen in the sky. Night would afford no adequate cover of darkness for any escape. 'Good ten hours before the moon goes down,' he muttered.

The report of another rifle shot sounded, but no bullet struck anywhere close. 'Different rifle,' Cotton muttered. 'Now what's goin' on?'

He waited, listening intently, for fifteen minutes. The sudden silence was accentuated, rather than relieved, by normal sounds, near and distant.

An eagle screamed, floating high in the sky. Deer flies buzzed around his head. In the distance, normal herd noises from the cattle and yells of the drovers marked their location. Cows bawled for their calves, each finding and nursing her own as she prepared to settle down for the night. Somewhere behind him, a small animal scurried through dry brush with soft, scuffing sounds. Beyond that, no sound offered any clue to what was happening beyond his tiny circle of restricted vision.

Then a familiar voice called, 'You takin' a nap or just hidin' out till the chores is done.'

Relief flooded through him as he recognized Cap Lindiken's drawl. 'Keep your head down, Cap!' he called back without raising his own. 'There's a bushwhacker on the hill.'

'Naw, not no more there ain't,' Cap replied with an exaggerated drawl. 'You can stand up and stretch any time you take a notion.'

Cotton risked a look over the top of the tree trunk. Cap sat his horse thirty yards away. His right leg was hooked around the saddle horn. His hands were busy rolling a cigarette. He looked as relaxed as if reporting the return of a missing cow.

'What happened?' Cotton demanded.

'Aw, I heard some shootin', so I went and poked my nose in to find out what was goin' on. I seen he had you pinned down pretty tight there. I found a spot where I could get a good bead on him.'

'You get him?'

'He didn't try to shoot back, anyhow.'

'Who was he?'

'One of our own hands.'

'One of our own hands?' Cotton echoed incredulously.

Cap nodded. 'Guy that called himself Will Smith. The Texan.'

'Why was he gunnin' for me?'

Cap leaned forward, resting his forearm on the saddle horn. His droll reply was offered with no change of expression. 'Well now, I asked him exactly that. He didn't offer me any explanation at all. Of course, that might have somethin' to do with the fact that

I'd done shot him already before I thought to ask.'

With an equally straight face, Cotton replied, 'Well, next time see if you can get some answers first, before you go shootin' folks.'

'I'll try to keep that in mind,' Cap assured him.

In Cotton's mind, there was no need for the question anyway. What he really wondered was how many more of the crew he had hired were there only for a chance to kill him. It was not a comfortable thought, with 600 miles of trail ahead.

It was almost an hour later when he looked Cap up to thank him for saving his life.

8

Nothing is ever as easy as it sounds. Moving a herd of 1,500 cattle, more than a dozen wagons, and a good-sized company of people was no different.

Lame horses, too sore to keep up, had to be abandoned.

Half a dozen cows were snake-bitten, and had to be shot.

One cowboy, thrown from his horse, struck his head against a rock and was killed. They buried him near where he fell. A wooden marker, his name carved into it with a knife, was placed at his grave. Even as they did so, they all knew full well it would be gone within a year. The ceaseless high prairie winds would first scour the name away. Then rain and snow would finish the destruction of the wood. Forever after, the winds would blow across the forgotten grave as if it never were.

The sandhills were more of a challenge than anticipated. They extended a hundred miles further west than anyone had remembered. Unable to skirt them as planned, they had to move the herd through almost forty miles of their seeming endless, rolling hills of fine sand, covered with only a thin layer of sod.

The grass was good, so the cattle fared well. The wagons, however, bogged down in soft mud in the low spots between hills. They stirred up rancid, black muck that grasped and clung to the narrow wheels. Over the tops of the endless hills those wheels often broke through the shallow sod and sank into the fine sand. Teams had to be doubled on the wagons, just to drag them through. Some days saw less than two or three miles of progress.

By the time they reached the Niobrara River, they had begun to think the sand would never end. The Niobrara presented its own challenge, with the spring run-off transforming a normal stream into a raging torrent that had to be crossed. Ropes were strung across to tether wagons as they were floated into the turbulent flood. It seemed a small miracle that they all crossed without being ripped apart by the force of the surging waters.

Beyond the Niobrara, the hard, white clay offered a much welcomed change. Grass was still plentiful, but the search for adequate water for each night's camp became increasingly difficult. Even so, their progress improved significantly. The cattle adjusted to the schedule and rigors of the drive. Wagons moved more easily. Even the hot sun and seemingly endless winds failed to dampen their enthusiasm.

It was a welcome respite, but too good to remain true for long. The euphoria of conquering miles of trouble-free country collapsed abruptly.

Cotton spotted the swiftly moving cloud of dust, small though it was. He reined in, studying its advance. His stomach tightened into a knot. His jaw tensed. 'That's a horse, runnin' flat out.

Somebody's spotted trouble,' he muttered softly.

He nudged his horse to the top of the hill, where the approaching rider could spot him swiftly and easily. He was rewarded by the almost instant adjustment in the movement of the dust, turning directly toward him.

In minutes, the form at the front of that dust became discernible. He recognized Tim McGhghy (he pronounced it, 'Mc Gahay'), one of the hands from the Holland ranch. He was bent forward over the saddle horn, reducing his wind drag as much as possible. The brim on the front of his hat was blown up against the crown. With every stride he nudged his lathered horse to greater effort.

Still 200 yards from Cotton, he began to yell. 'Indians! There's a whole swarm of 'em!'

'Where?' Cotton demanded.

Two other hands, seeing the urgency of Tim's approach, had galloped within earshot. Tim pointed north and east.

'About three miles. Maybe a little more.'

'How many?'

'Gotta be a hundred! Maybe more. They got us spotted. They're headin' straight for us.'

Cap Lindiken had also spotted the runner's dust. He galloped up, his horse braking to a stiff-legged, jolting halt. 'What's up?' he demanded.

'Big bunch of Indians north and east. Tim says they've already got us spotted.'

'They had to've spotted us yesterday already,' Tim opined, talking fast and excitedly. 'I got a real good look at 'em. They're armed to the teeth. No women or kids. Just warriors. All decked out in war paint. Lord, do they look fearsome!'

'Did they see you?' Cap demanded.

Tim shook his head. 'I don't think so. I was scoutin', like I'm supposed to be doin'. I was just about ready to ride outa the edge of some trees, when I spotted 'em, down in the valley. I'm pretty sure I ducked back afore they had a chance to see me. Got a real good look at 'em, though.'

Cap turned to Cotton. 'If there's that many, they aren't plannin' on just tryin' to run off a few head of stock. They're plannin' on wipin' out the whole outfit. They want 'em all, and the horses and mules too.'

Cotton's look was grim. 'Sounds like it. Looks like we're in for a fight.'

He turned to one of the hands who had ridden up when Tim first arrived. 'Leonard, you get to the wagons. Tell 'em to get 'em circled right around the top of that knoll yonder. That'll give us a clear field o' fire all the way around. Tell 'em to get set for an all-out battle.'

He turned to another cowboy. 'Slim, you get word around the herd, for everybody to leave the cattle and get to the wagons. The wagons will be well ahead, between the cattle and the Indians. They'll deal with us before they worry about them. We'll round up the cattle that scatter later.'

He turned back to Tim. 'Tim, you head to the remuda. Get a fresh horse, and tell the wranglers to get the horses and mules back behind the herd, and keep their heads up. The Indians won't likely go for the horses, either, until they have a go at us. Tell 'em if any of the Indians do come at 'em, leave the horses and hightail it for the wagons. Horses an' mules ain't worth them gettin' themselves killed for.'

Tim rode off, coaxing his exhausted horse to a lope. 'They'll most likely be wantin' to palaver afore they try anything,' Cap suggested.

Cotton nodded. 'They'll be Pawnee, I'd guess,' he replied. 'Kinda far north for them, but too far south for Sioux. Not that it matters a whole lot.'

'Arapaho, most likely,' Cap corrected. 'But you're right. It don't matter none at this point.'

The two rode toward the already circling wagons at a lope. They supervised the location of the wagons. They helped unload things large enough to provide shelter between and beneath wagons. Everyone pitched in feverishly, as they prepared for battle.

With amazing speed the wagons were arranged evenly around the top of the large knoll. Teams were unhooked from their wagons and herded to the center of the large circle. There they were securely tethered to prevent their running away or trampling anyone in their fear.

Cap personally arranged the location of his mystery wagon. It alone kept its team in harness. It was faced inward toward the center of the circle, so the back of the wagon was directed toward the oncoming foe.

Cotton scowled as Sarge Winthrop grinned in response to something Cap said. 'He's been around enough scrapes to know this ain't a laughin' matter,' he complained to himself.

'There they come,' somebody yelled.

As if in response, an increasingly large body of Indians appeared over the crest of a broad hill. They were spread out into a line a quarter-mile long. Behind the front of the line more warriors continued to come into view.

'Spaced out real good to look impressive,' Cap commented.

'Gettin' the job done, too,' Cotton responded. 'I'm pertneart impressed enough to wet my pants.'

'They'll stop in about half a minute, and a couple of 'em will ride out front to palaver.'

As if listening to his comments for instructions, the Indians did exactly that. As soon as the whole party of warriors was visible, they stopped. Two of them, from almost the exact center of the line, kicked their horses into a trot. They rode fifty yards in front of the rest, and stopped, clearly waiting for a response.

Cotton rode out between two of the wagons, followed by Cap. Cap moved up beside Cotton as they moved away from the shelter of the wagons. They rode about fifty yards, then they, too, stopped.

'That's far enough until they move. Make 'em come to us,' Cotton said softly.

The spokesmen of the Indians were obviously hesitant to do so. They sat their horses where they were, trying to out-wait their intended victims. When Cotton and Cap refused to take the bait, they reluctantly began to move slowly forward. As they did, Cotton and Cap moved forward as well, matching their pace to that of the Indians, moving no faster than they moved, ensuring they would meet no more than halfway between the two forces, well out of range of the waiting warriors.

Twice the Indians slowed, waiting for the white men to travel the greater distance. Each time, Cap and Cotton slowed as well. In the end, they met almost exactly halfway between.

The frown on the Indian spokesman's face betrayed his frustration and anger at having his tactic fail. He spoke, in surprisingly good English. 'You intrude on Arapaho land.'

Keeping his face impassive, his voice even, Cotton responded: 'We pass through land that lies open before us. It is not the normal land of the Arapaho. We have no intention to harm any of your people.'

'You intrude on the land of the Arapaho,' the obvious chief repeated. 'We will take two hundred of your cattle and fifty of your horses to allow you to pass.'

'We offer no cattle and no horses,' Cotton replied. 'We wish to pass in peace. Whether we do so depends on you. If we are not allowed to pass in peace, we will leave many of your lodges empty of men.'

The chief's eyes flashed. 'Big words for so small a company of men. I have ten warriors for every one of your men.'

'That ain't enough,' Cotton answered, as if discussing the weather. 'If you want a battle, you better have at least twenty to one.'

The chief was at a complete loss for words for several heartbeats. When he could control his anger enough to speak evenly, he said, 'We will see if you can fight as well as you can talk. And when we have finished the taking of your scalps we will take our fill of your women before we scalp them as well.'

'Well, I guess you'll just have to come and get 'em if you think you can,' Cotton taunted.

Without replying, the two Indians wheeled their horses and galloped back toward their line. Cap and Cotton did the same, racing toward the wagons.

'Did you have to go and deliberately taunt 'em that way?' Cap complained.

'Yup,' Cotton responded, bent low over his saddle horn. 'I wanted to make 'em mad enough to come chargin' straight at us.'

The war whoops and yells behind them confirmed the effectiveness of the plan.

As the pair raced between wagons to the shelter of the circle, Cap swerved aside, riding toward Sarge Winthrop. Cotton yelled, 'Everybody get set, but don't fire a shot till I say so!'

Rifles levered cartridges into firing chambers all along the line of wagons. Cotton called three men by name, instructing them, 'You three get over to the other sides of the circle. Make sure they don't send a hidden bunch to circle around behind us.'

The three sprinted to their assigned post.

Riding close beside each other, the Indians raced toward them, yelling at the top of their voices. The cumulative effect of so many, yelling so loudly, was an absolutely blood-curdling sound. Try as they might to ignore it, it still sent fear surging into the gut of every defender of the wagons. Trying to counter the fear, Cotton constantly said, in an exaggeratedly calm and steady voice, 'Hold your fire. Hold your fire.'

The nearer the screaming, whooping Indians drew, the harder it was for those under attack to comply. Nevertheless, they did. By the time they were a hundred yards distant, arrows were flying. Bullets were whizzing past, or thunking into the hastily assembled defenses. Then Cotton yelled, 'Now! Fire!'

Instantly a withering fire erupted from wagons. It was effective, but against such a large number of assailants it was instantly obvious that it would be inadequate.

Above the noise of battle Cap's voice yelled, 'Now, Sarge!'

In response, Sarge Winthrop stood and whipped aside a tarpaulin that had been draped across the mystery object in the back of Cap's mystery wagon. With a roar, Sarge grabbed the handle of the suddenly exposed Gatling gun and began to turn it. Directing the stream of deadly fire, he swept it across the advancing face of the attacking horde.

It took several seconds for the charging Indians to realize what it was they faced. In those seconds, Indians and horses alike collapsed as if some giant scythe swept their feet from under them.

The war whoops of the attackers changed tone at once. They became cries of surprise and fear, followed by an almost eerie silence as they attempted to wheel their horses to flee.

Over the rhythmic, five-per-second reports of the Gatling gun, only the screams and cries of dying horses and men could be heard. The searing hail of death swept the charging tide back as fearsomely as if an angel of death had swept a superhuman hand across the hillside.

The occupants of the wagons stared in open-mouthed surprise at least as great as the victims of the slaughter. Forgotten guns lay quiet in stupefied hands. Fully half of the attacking Indians lay dead or dying on the ground. The survivors fled, pursued by the incessant bark of the death-spewing weapon of destruction.

Over its hammering, an almost insane battle cry roared from the throat of its operator. Almost at his side to be heard, at the top of his voice, Cap yelled, 'Sarge! Cease fire!'

Slowly the words penetrated the seasoned warrior's battle craze. His hand slowed and stopped. He closed his mouth. He stared at the carnage stretched before him, as if seeing it for the first time. 'Let it cool,' Cap commanded. 'You'll melt the barrel down.'

Sarge opened his mouth to speak and closed it again. In a voice sounding suddenly small and timid, he said, 'I got a couple extra barrels.'

Cotton was already moving along the line of wagons, checking for casualties. Miraculously, there were two minor wounds only. He began to bark orders.

'Let's get the teams hitched up again. Let's move on. We'll back off to where the herd is for the night. Let the Indians come and gather their dead and wounded. Double the guards on cattle and horses both tonight. I don't think they'll come back, but we'll be ready if they do.'

He wasn't sure whether he was more eager to get past Arapaho country, or to escape the image of the price their victory had exacted. Maybe the whispering grapevine of the plains would send word ahead of them that would prevent their need to use such an instrument of self-defense again. He could only hope.

9

'Mr Lang, sir?'

Cotton turned and looked down. Little Timothy McGhghy waited for his response. At five years old, the boy's thatch of red hair perfectly matched the color of the prolific freckles just beginning to become prominent across his face. He was the eldest son of Tim and Ramona McGhghy, one of Holland's hands.

'Hey, Slipsaddle,' Cotton teased, using his favorite nickname for the boy. 'Are you OK?'

Looking overly serious, the boy did not offer his usual response to the name. Instead, he said, 'Mr Lang, can I tell you somethin', without bein' a tattle-tail?'

The thought of half a dozen things needing immediate attention vied with the boy's request for several seconds.

Sensing his seriousness, however, Cotton squatted down to the boy's level. 'Sure, Timmy. What's up?'

'Well, I ain't right sure, Mr. Lang, but I think I seen something maybe you oughta know about.'

'What's that, Timmy?'

'Well, it was just when them Indians was a-comin' at us, and screamin' an' hollerin' and all.'

When he failed to continue, Cotton sought to encourage him. 'Yes? And . . . ?'

Timmy swallowed hard and looked around, as if afraid of being overheard. 'Well, Pa, he stuck me inside the wagon, and told me to keep my head down. He'll likely whup me if he finds out. I couldn't see what was goin' on from there. A guy really needs to know what's goin' on,' he defended, almost truculently.

'OK,' Cotton hesitated. 'And then what?'

'Well, sir, I sorta slipped outa the wagon so I could see. I seen one of the men in our bunch that wasn't aimin' his gun at the Indians.'

Cotton's attention level leaped instantly. 'What do you mean?'

'Well sir,' Timmy repeated, as if it were a litany demanding use with every sentence, 'He was aimin' his gun at where you was.'

'At me?'

'Well sir, Mr Lang, it sure 'nough looked like it to me. He was pointin' right at where you was standin'. But just then that there other gun started makin' that God-awful . . . uh, I mean, that really loud racket it makes, and everybody stopped shootin' and got real quiet, just watchin'. The man pointin' his gun at you said some words Ma says I shouldn't never say, and put his gun down.'

Cotton frowned as he realized the import of the child's words. 'Then what did he do, Timmy?'

Timmy shrugged his young shoulders. 'He just sort of walked off where he could see what the Indians was doin'.'

Cotton processed the information for

several seconds. 'Do you know the man's name, Timmy?'

'Well sir, yes sir. I heard my pa say his name a couple times. My pa doesn't like him, I don't think. Anyway, he says his name like he doesn't like him. He told my ma that he doesn't think it's probably his real name anyway, and she should watch out and be careful of him. He thinks Ma's real pretty, even if she is awful old. I think she's already thirty or sixty or somethin' really old like that.'

Cotton stifled his impatience. 'What's his name, Timmy?'

'Well sir, it's Mr. Houston. His name is Hank Houston.'

The name clicked instantly with Cotton. Hank Houston and Will Smith, the man who had tried to bushwhack him, had both worked for Dugger before signing on with the drive. They were almost always together, before Cap had shot Smith.

Cotton took a deep breath. He stood up, stretching his legs. 'Thank you, Timmy,' he said. 'That is a really important thing for me to know. Knowing it just might save my life.'

'You ain't gonna tell my pa I sneaked out of the wagon, are you?' Timmy worried.

Cotton resisted the urge to smile. 'Well, no, I guess not. It'll be our secret this time. But after this, you need to do what your pa tells you to. Understand? You could have been killed, then what would your folks do?'

Timmy shrugged. His answer was very matter-of-fact. 'They'd just have to have another kid to take my place,' he said. 'I think they prob'ly will anyway.'

Again Cotton resisted the smile that threatened to break out. With great seriousness, he said, 'It doesn't really work that way, Timmy. Even having another boy would never take the place of having you. They'd be sad for the whole rest of their lives if something happened to you.'

'Do you really think so?'

'I'm sure of it. Now you best get back to your wagon. And thank you.'

Without another word, the boy turned and left on a dead run.

Cotton was still standing there, pondering his options, when a hue and cry from the distance snatched his attention.

Mule teams had been rehitched to their respective wagons. They were strung out single file, heading for the designated spot to camp, away from the carnage of the battle mound.

Will Seaberg was a top-notch horse wrangler and rough string rider. Instead of using his name, everyone simply called him 'Rawhide'. It was he who approached at a dead run. At the first of the wagons he slowed, shouting to the driver. The driver leaned out around the side of his wagon and waved a hand in Cotton's direction.

Instantly the wrangler clamped the spurs to his horse and headed to where Cotton waited.

Before he arrived Cap trotted to his side. 'Trouble with the horses,' he surmised.

Cotton held his tongue, waiting for whatever message the wrangler brought so urgently. As he skidded his horse to a stiff-legged, jarring halt, Cotton enquired, 'What's goin' on, Rawhide?'

'They got the kid!' Seaberg exclaimed.

An icy chill settled through Cotton's body. His voice betrayed his dismay and apprehension. 'Rusty?'

Rawhide nodded emphatically. 'Yeah. Him and a dozen or so horses.'

'What happened?' Cotton demanded.

'They busted off half a dozen warriors when they attacked the wagons. Sent 'em around in a big circle, around the herd. They was after horses, figgerin' everybody'd be with the wagons, fixin' to fight. We was just tryin' to keep the horses from gettin' too excited, when they come bustin' outa a bunch o' trees, yellin' an' hollerin' an' shootin'. They got Rusty's horse right off. It dumped him when it went down. One o' them Indians reached down an' grabbed 'im on a dead run. Whipped 'im up on his horse. Musta pertneart tore his arm outa

102

the socket. I seen Rusty tryin' to fight, and the Indian clubbed him over the head. Rusty just flopped down across the horse. Musta plumb knocked 'im out. They got a dozen or so horses an' Rusty, an' they hightailed it. Me'n Shorty was shootin' at 'em, but tryin' not to hit the kid. I think we mighta winged one or two, but they got plumb away.'

Alf Fankhouser's face filled Cotton's memory. His eyes pleaded, as his words echoed in Cotton's mind, '*You'll take good care of the boy? His ma'll die if anything happens to him.*'

He looked at Cap Lindiken. 'We gotta go get 'im,' he said.

Cap nodded as if it were the most natural thing in the world. 'We'd best get a couple extra guns an' ammunition outa the wagon.'

He turned back to Seaberg. 'Rawhide, I want a horse saddled to take with us for Rusty to ride back. Stick a halter over his bridle, so I can lead him at a run.'

Rawhide nodded wordlessly and

wheeled his mount. As if by some prearranged choreograph, he and Cap turned their horses and loped to the lead wagon, driven by Chet Holland.

'What's up now?' Chet demanded, hauling his team of mules to a halt.

'Half a dozen Indians run off some of our horses,' Cotton explained hurriedly. 'They got Rusty Fankhouser.'

'The kid?'

'Yeah. Me'n Cap are goin' after him.'

Chet's mouth worked like a fish gasping for water for several seconds. 'You're what?'

'We gotta go get 'im,' Cotton repeated.

'You're gonna ride after them Indians?'

Cotton took a deep breath. Cap was already in the wagon, grabbing the extra guns and ammunition their mission would demand. 'I promised his dad I'd take care of the boy,' he explained. 'I stuck him back with the horses, thinking he'd be safe there. I was wrong. He wasn't. Now I gotta go get 'im back.'

'You can't just go bustin' after a bunch o' Indians on the warpath!'

'I ain't got a choice,' Cotton argued. 'I ain't gonna be able to live with myself if I don't. They ain't likely to be expectin' anyone to come chasin' 'em anyway.'

'Why, that's, that's . . . that's just plumb nuts! What am I gonna do for a trail boss if both of you go gettin' yourselves killed?'

Cap emerged from the wagon. He handed Cotton a forty-five in a holster. Its belt was filled with cartridges. Cotton ducked his head through its loop and draped it across his shoulder. Then Cap handed him a rifle and a double-barreled shotgun. A canvas bag filled with ammunition, with two loops for handles, came next. Cotton dropped the handles over his saddle horn and took the two long weapons.

Similarly armed, Cap mounted. Cotton turned back to the herd's owner. 'If we don't make it back, Leonard McConnell will make you a good trail boss,' he said.

With no further talk, they lifted their horses to a lope. They were met within a quarter of a mile by Will Seaberg. He held the lead rope of an extra horse. It was saddled. The reins of the bridle were knotted around the saddle horn. Over the bridle, a halter held the lead rope by which he led the extra mount. 'I'm comin' with you,' he announced as they approached.

Cotton only nodded. 'Show us their trail.'

In less than thirty minutes they were following the clearly defined trail of the fleeing Indians with the stolen horses. They rode at a lope for three miles, before Cotton signaled for them to slow.

'We're gettin' over close to the river. Their camp can't be too far off, I'm guessin'. We'd best start movin' more careful.'

Wordlessly the other two complied. They hugged the low ground, making use of every bit of available cover. Three sets of eyes fearfully watched the hilltops for any movement. Each time they were forced to cross high or open ground, they did so swiftly, scurrying to whatever cover afforded itself on the other side.

'Smoke yonder,' Cap breathed.

All three reined in, looking where he pointed. Moments later they, too, saw a small tendril of smoke appear briefly over the horizon, before it broke apart and drifted away on the breeze.

'Their camp?' Rawhide inquired softly.

'Most likely,' Cotton confirmed. 'You 'spect they'll have lookouts?'

Cap shook his head. 'I doubt it. They got a passel o' wounds to lick, an' nobody'd be crazy enough to chase 'em clear back to their camp.'

'You think they'll wanta keep the kid, or use 'im to make up for all the men they lost tryin' to attack us?'

Cap shrugged. 'I don't know. With that red hair an' all, he'd make a fine prize for 'em to keep. If he was five years younger, I'd say that's what they'd do. But he's pertneart a man. An' they're bound to be madder'n a bunch o' hornets. That red hair'll make a fine scalp, too.'

'Yeah,' Cotton agreed.

As swiftly as silence allowed, they rode toward the Indian encampment. The closer they drew, the more smoke from their fires could be seen before it dissipated. When they thought themselves just over the hill from their camp, they dismounted. Cautiously, they crept up the hill, until they could see over the top.

Screened by small brush and tall grass, they had a clear view of the whole encampment. Fifty or more tepees were scattered randomly. Mostly women and children were evident, moving about. 'Where's the men?' Rawhide whispered.

'Don't know,' Cotton replied. 'There's Rusty, though.'

In the middle of one clear area, Rusty Fankhouser, unmistakable by his red hair, sat cross-legged. His hands appeared to be tied behind him, but he was otherwise unfettered. Half a dozen Indians sat a few feet away from him.

'Waitin' for the others to get back from wherever they are,' Cap guessed.

'Probably took most o' the squaws an' went back after their dead an' wounded, maybe,' Cotton offered.

'Good a guess as any,' Cap agreed. 'I sure hope you're right.'

'We ain't gonna get a better chance, regardless,' Cotton said.

Cap pointed carefully. 'See where that neck o' timber juts out there?'

'Yup.'

'If we slip up there afore anyone sees us, we can maybe come bustin' right through the middle o' the camp, grab the kid, an' hightail it into that draw on the other side. We maybe can get in an' out before they know what hit 'em.'

'Huh uh,' Cotton disagreed. 'If we do that, we'll be stuck in that draw. The only way out will be up over the top, or right back through the camp.'

Cap digested the thought. 'Yeah, I guess you're right. What, then?'

'When we grab Rusty, cut to the left,

around that bunch o' willows. They'll give us some cover, and we can head right back here.'

He turned to Seaberg. 'Rawhide, you take the extra horse and wait just in the edge o' that bunch o' pine trees over yonder. You can pick off anyone chasin' us, and make 'em turn back long enough to get Rusty on a horse.'

'I don't get to go in with you, huh?' Seaberg lamented.

'Somebody's gotta hold the extra horse,' Cotton reasoned.

'Well, bring along at least one of 'em chasin' you,' Rawhide requested.

The three wriggled backward from their vantage point. When they were well below line of sight from the encampment, they stood and hurried to their mounts. Rawhide led the extra mount and headed for his assigned post. Cotton and Cap made a circle, approaching the Indian camp through the trees.

Just inside the edge of the trees they stopped. Each loaded a shotgun and levered a shell into the chamber of his extra rifle. Each stuck his reins in his mouth, biting down hard on the leather straps. They looked at each other. Cotton nodded. Cap nodded in return.

Both men leaned forward and silently jammed their spurs into their horses' sides. Both mounts leaped forward. In three strides, both were running at full speed.

Dogs began to bark just as they reached the edge of the encampment. Some part of Cotton's mind marveled that none had sensed them and sent up an alarm before. Then there was no time to think of anything.

An Indian burst from a tepee just to Cotton's right. A blast from Cotton's shotgun sent the brave catapulting backward, out of sight. Another appeared from nowhere, rifle in hand. The shotgun's other barrel discharged into him.

To his left, Cotton noted that Cap's shotgun had also discharged twice. As one, the two tossed the now worthless weapons aside. Firing without aiming, they sent the group of seated warriors scurrying for cover, grabbing for their weapons.

With a cry of jubilance, Rusty Fankhouser leaped to his feet. Somehow, he had managed to free his hands from the fetters that bound them behind his back, without his captors noticing. As Cotton and Cap raced past, guns blazing, he reached upward.

Gripping his rifle in the other hand, Cotton grasped the boy's wrist. Rusty's hand closed around his wrist in a corresponding grip. Using the speed of the horse to assist his leap, Rusty sprang up, landing astride Cotton's horse, just behind the cantle. The horse flinched perceptibly at the sudden addition of weight, but adjusted at once.

In seconds they were around the patch of willows, out of sight of the village. Pandemonium erupted behind them.

Heedless of anything behind them, they spurred their horses toward the shelter of the trees. As they approached, Rawhide's rifle barked twice. Somewhere behind them a horse squealed in pain.

Rawhide was mounted, holding the mount for Rusty. He had already removed the halter and lead rope. As Rusty slid from Cotton's horse and sprinted toward the one brought for him, Rawhide flipped him the reins.

Without a word the four thundered out the other side of the trees, fleeing for their lives. 'How many behind us?' Cotton called to Rawhide.

'I seen five,' Rawhide called back. 'Danged if I know how they got to their horses that quick! I knocked one off his horse an' shot the horse out from under another. The rest turned back. They didn't know how many was waitin' in the trees.'

'They'll be comin',' Cotton predicted.

It was one of the few times he remembered being glad he was wrong. For whatever reason, pursuit from the Indian encampment never materialized. After running their horses for a mile, they slowed, listening for the pursuit that never came.

From a spot they deemed secure, they stopped and watched their back trail for several minutes. 'You reckon they ain't even gonna try to catch us?' Cap marveled.

Cotton took a deep breath. 'Looks thataway. Maybe between losin' half their warriors in the attack, what's left in camp ain't got the heart for it.'

Cap chuckled suddenly. 'I betcha they figure we've got that there Gatlin' gun set up somewhere here, an' we're tryin' to sucker 'em into chasin' us right into it.'

The further from the encampment they traveled, and the closer to their wagons, the greater the sense of relief in Cotton grew. The celebration when they rejoined the wagons was muted in comparison to his own jubilation.

In his excitement, Timmy's warning about Hank Houston got shoved into the back of his mind. It would be a costly lapse.

10

Summer caught up with them with a vengeance. They crossed into Dakota Territory. Lakota country. Sioux. The word itself made the back of Cotton's neck tingle. Water grew continually more scarce. The grass was ample, from extraordinarily good spring rains, but it was already turning brown and dry in the summer heat and wind. In the wake of the herd, 6,000 individual hoofs had churned it to powder that drifted and hung in the air.

Talk of being able to feast on buffalo meat had turned to talk of the absence of buffalo. They still hadn't seen a single one of the fabled animals. All the trail gossip he had ever heard indicated there should be almost numberless thousands of them on these plains. There was not one.

They encountered other people every

few days. Occasional trappers, prospec-
tors, drifters, small groups of Indians,
and sometimes soldiers broke the
endless monotony of the drive. Each
offered a chance to catch up on gossip,
hear stories that hadn't already grown
trite and stale, and gain valuable
information on what lay ahead. Almost
everyone they encountered seemed to
know about their confrontation with the
Arapaho. Their 'big gun that talks fast'
was on the lips of everyone, it seemed.

Cotton wiped the back of his hand
across his dirt-encrusted lips, pressed
tightly together. He swiped the back of
the hand absent-mindedly across his
chaps. It left a streak of darker, slightly
damp dirt across the weathered leather.

His eyes squinted into the distance. If
he could have seen a mirror, he'd have
laughed at his own appearance. Those
squinting eyes seemed to peer from
within two holes bored into an earthen
mask.

It was hot. Too hot. Sweat soaked his
shirt, darkened his hat from the

hatband halfway up the crown.

He was the trail boss. He could stay in the vanguard of the herd, let the drovers eat the dust. He just wasn't cut out that way. He took his turn riding drag with the rest.

And it was as dusty as it was hot. The ceaseless wind bore aloft every grain of dirt ripped loose by the hooves of the cattle. Each particle that touched his face stuck to the sweat, turned to mud, then dried. By this time of day it had formed a mask of earth that covered every exposed piece of skin. His eyes made two holes in that mask. His mouth another, in a straight, tight line beneath his somewhat large nose.

He turned his head, pushed his right nostril shut with an index finger, and blew his nose explosively. A wad of dark mud, expelled by the effort, shot outward. He turned his head the other way and did the same with the other nostril.

Each time, his horse's ears twitched at the sudden explosion of air. The iron-gray gelding gave no other indication of attention to the detail of personal grooming.

Cotton inhaled deeply. He gave a slight nod of approval to the improved air flow through his nose.

As he squinted across the moving backs of 1,500 head of cattle, his experienced eye caught their change of attitude instantly. Starting with those furthest from him, noses lifted a shade higher into the air. Tails that were sagging straight down or swishing at pesky insects lifted slightly. The pace of tired hoofs picked up perceptibly.

Then the horse caught it too. His ears shot forward. His head bobbed up and down twice as his nostrils flared.

The rider smiled tightly. He knew the signs. He knew he'd be able to smell it pretty soon, himself. He lifted his own head in anticipation.

In a hot, dry summer, the smell of water on the breeze is unmistakable. When it has been two days of trailing and camping without the precious substance, it was magic. Like electricity, it radiated through the herd. In seconds their reluctant, ambling shuffle changed to a brisk walk, then lifted to a trot. The lead riders had already fanned out to the sides of the herd, knowing they could neither slow nor stop them now until they reached the cool relief of the water they had smelled.

He didn't need to eat the continuous dirt that riding drag always included any longer. He lifted the reins and turned the horse at right angles to the herd. He knew the lie of the country from the crude map Holland had drawn. He well knew the broad stream they approached. He also knew it was a vital source of water for several tribes of Lakota.

He and his thirsty horse encountered that stream nearly half a mile upstream from the herd. Neither horse nor man hesitated. He rode directly into the water until the animal was knee deep. He slid out of the saddle into the sudden shock of cold water as the gelding lowered his muzzle into the delicious fluid that flowed around him.

The rider let him drink for a moment, then pulled up on the bridle strap, forcing the animal to lift his head. 'Don't overdo it, fella,' he said softly. 'You're purty hot. Don't want ya founderin'.'

The gelding failed to understand. He shook his head against the restraint, wanting to fill his belly with the icy refreshment, unaware that he could kill himself doing so. He resisted as much as his training would allow as the man led him back out of the stream and several yards away from its edge.

He looked back longingly at the rushing stream for a moment, then resigned himself to tearing off large mouthfuls of the verdant grass growing in the river's proximity.

Leaving the reins dropped on the ground, the rider walked back to the water's edge. He knelt on the bank and removed his hat. He looked in all directions for a long moment, then rinsed off his hands. Making a bowl of his cupped hands, he lifted water to his mouth and drank greedily.

Between each handful of water, he glanced quickly in all direction, ensuring himself that he was alone.

He returned to the horse and led him back to the water, letting him drink again. This time the animal was not as avidly eager. When he had drawn in another hefty drink, Cotton led him away from the stream again.

Leaving his mount, he walked upstream twenty yards and walked back into the river. He untied the leather thong that held the bottom of the holster of the Colt forty-five. He unbuckled the gun belt, removed it from around his waist, then refastened the buckle. He looped it over his head so it hung on a shoulder, with the gun itself at shoulder level, positioned where he could grasp the well-worn walnut grips instantly. Then he waded further into the water.

A stream of muddy water flowed from him downstream, as the caked dust and dirt was washed from his clothing.

In the center of the stream he removed his hat and washed the dirt from it. He looked around carefully again. Lifting the holstered gun high above his head with one hand, holding his hat in the other, he plunged into the icy torrent, then stood, shaking his head.

He looked around again, then repeated the process several more times, always careful to keep the holstered Colt well above the water.

He had turned and started back toward his horse when he saw him. He cursed silently, but managed to betray no surprise by action or expression. He was certain the Indian had been watching him every minute. Even so, he had ridden nearly to the edge of the stream before Cotton saw him.

They stared at each other for nearly two minutes. It was the Indian who eventually spoke. 'You are the one called Cotton.'

Cotton nodded almost imperceptibly. 'An' I reckon you'd be Grey Wolf.'

'I have heard much of you,' the Indian replied.

'Heard a mite about you, too, as a matter of fact,' Cotton replied. 'You're a tad far south, ain't ya?'

The Indian's expression didn't change. 'I am Grey Wolf. I ride and I hunt where I wish. Where do you go with the cattle?'

'We're just movin' through,' Cotton offered. 'Headin' toward Montana Territory with 'em.'

'I was told the man with the long scar was a warrior, not a cattleman. They are your cattle?'

Cotton resisted the urge to run a finger down the faint scar that ran down from his forehead, across his left eye, past his nose, across the end of his mouth, all the way down to his chin. 'Some of 'em. Not the rest. Just hired on. Thought I'd see some new country.'

'You will be in the country of the Crow when you get to where you are going.'

'Yeah, that's troubled me some. We'll be passin' through your people's huntin' grounds afore that, though.'

'Our hunting ground is not good this year. The buffalo have not come. It is past their time.'

'That ain't good. I don't guess us passin' through will make 'em any later, though.'

'If I let you live to do that.'

'Well, you can always make a stab at stoppin' us. I've heard you're a great warrior.'

Cotton thought there was just a flicker in the impassive eyes that surveyed him, but it was there for only the barest of instants. 'And I have heard that of you as well. I have heard that you emptied the tepees of many, many Arapaho. You counted coup enough to earn at least three eagle feathers when you took your young man back from the middle of their camp. It was a feat worthy of the best Lakota warrior. Perhaps we will find which of us is the greater warrior before these cattle have eaten so much of my people's grass that the buffalo will stay away.'

'We just might at that, but I'd rather not.'

The Lakota warrior wheeled his horse and galloped swiftly away. He was scarcely gone when Cap trotted out of the cottonwoods and approached Cotton. Cotton waded out onto the bank of the stream. He carefully dried the inside of his holster, then replaced the gun and holster around his waist. He sat down on a large rock and removed his boots. As he dumped the water from them, wrung out his socks and replaced them, Cap asked, 'Was that Grey Wolf?'

Cotton nodded. 'That was him.'

'I thought it looked like the descriptions I've heard. I take it ya kept your six gun with ya whilst ya was takin' yer Sunday bath.'

'It seemed like a good idea at the time.'

'It'd be a better idea if 'n ya'd pair up with someone. Let one watch whilst t'other warshes.'

'Yeah. Might be at that.'

'So why didn't ya shoot him?'

'It crossed my mind.'

'And?'

'What would you've done?'

'That all depends. I ain't as quick on the draw as you.'

'I had my gun clear up by my shoulder.'

'You ain't so quick with it up there, huh?'

'I don't know. Never had to find out. I wasn't none too keen on findin' out against Grey Wolf, neither. I've heard stories about that one. Besides, he hadn't given me any reason to try.'

'Do ya know what that man can do?'

'I mighta heard. Tell me anyway.'

'I heard from a fella that claimed to see 'im do it. He can fire off an arrow at somethin' fifty yards away, grab another arrow, fit it to his bow, aim, an' fire the second arrow, an' the second arrow'll be fired afore the first one gets to what he's shootin' at. An' a third one'll be in the air afore the second one hits. If 'n it's a fella he's shootin' at, the second an' third ones'll be aimed at first one side, then the other, o' where the guy was when the shootin' started. That way, in case the guy steps to one side as he starts to shoot back, Grey Wolf'll git 'im anyhow.'

'That's pretty much what I heard too. Along with some other stuff, half o' which prob'ly ain't true.'

'But you ain't sure which half?'

'That's the problem. And I ain't aimin' to find out, if I don't hafta. If even half of what I've heard is true, if I'd grabbed for my gun, he'da been hangin' down on one side of his horse or the other before I coulda hauled it out, shootin' at me from under the horse's neck. I mighta got 'im, but he mighta got me at the same time. No, if I gotta go up against 'im, I'd just as soon wait for a lot better time an' place.'

Cap nodded. 'I 'spect that's exactly the reason he didn't try to kill you while he had the chance as well.'

Cotton nodded, knowing it was probably true.

11

The constant wind made it bearable, but just barely. At least it evaporated the sweat a little faster, for whatever cooling that offered.

The sun beat down relentlessly on the parched, rolling prairie. The lush grass, stirrup high, rustled drily as the wind rocked it back and forth. Its throaty, rustling voice sounded to Cotton like arid, rasped pleas for water, whispered from a million thirsty stalks.

The uncommonly abundant spring rains had brought prolific growth to the grass. Then, with the summer heat came the ceaseless winds. They sucked all the green from the grass and left it standing dry and brown, stretching endlessly across the hills. The hot wind sapped moisture from ground and grass alike until it crunched and crackled with each step of his horse's hoofs.

Cotton rode alertly, his restless eyes moving constantly near and far. He didn't need to be the one riding scout, any more than he needed to take his turn riding drag. He was, after all, the trail boss. He could stay with the herd, or with the wagons, or where the danger was less. In reality, though, he couldn't. He could not, would not, ask any of his men to do a job he himself was unwilling to take a turn doing.

Riding scout was easily the most dangerous task that fell to any of the crew. It was the scout who would first encounter any of the half-dozen lethal dangers of Dakota Territory. It was also the scout whom either marauding Indians or larcenous outlaws would try to eliminate first, to provide themselves with the advantage of surprise.

Cotton was a good five miles ahead and east of the herd. It was the direction from which his greatest concern emanated. They had yet to encounter any substantial number of Lakotas, and he knew they were in the area. He also knew the buffalo were uncommonly late migrating this far north. Their tardiness, he assumed, was due, at least in part, to the richly plentiful grass. That made it easier for them to keep their bellies full without moving as far or fast. That also made the cattle herd especially enticing to Indians worried about winter food and protective hides.

From just below the crest of a tall ridge he scanned the country carefully. He spotted pronghorn antelope, mule deer, a few elk, and several coyotes. Nothing else moved.

Just before he nudged his horse forward, he turned and glanced back over his shoulder. He froze in place instantly. His face drained of color. He rose in the stirrups, stretching to see better.

Swearing under his breath, he prodded his horse on to the top of the ridge where he could see better. He swore again.

It was easily a mile away, but that was

much, much too close. A bank of smoke, stretching more than a mile in length, boiled up from the ground. It blossomed red at its base. Fierce flames rolled upward into banks of swirling smoke. The clouds of smoke rose upward, lit from within as if with the fires of hell itself. He watched in horror as it visibly grew, fanned by the ceaseless winds.

He looked to left and right. No haven from the furious onslaught was visible in any direction.

He wheeled his horse down off the ridge. He didn't need spurs. The horse had seen what he had seen, had smelled the raging death riding the wings of the wind. Ears laid back against his head, he hit full stride before the bottom of the ridge. As the ground flattened out, so did his pace. The tall, rustling grass turned to a blur as man and animal raced for their lives.

Half a mile later Cotton glanced over his shoulder. The fire was closer! It was moving faster than his horse could run.

Nothing on earth is as terrifying as a prairie fire in tall grass, spurred by high winds. Nothing else is as totally, mindlessly merciless.

In the face of the racing inferno, every form of wildlife fled in utter terror. None but a scant few of the very fleetest had any hope whatever.

A rabbit scurried through the grass, not bothering to duck and dodge as was his normal pattern. He ran in a straight line, seeking only to escape as fast as he could flee. A large hawk spotted him and swept down in a steep dive. His talons gripped the unexpectedly easy meal and swept it off the ground. His great wings began a frantic beat to bear his prey up and away. He badly underestimated the speed and ferocity of the raging fire. Prey and predator were incinerated together, dying instantly in midair, exploding into a single ball of flame that disappeared into the barreling wall of fire.

An antelope doe and fawn fled together. The fawn fell back a few paces, unable to keep up with its mother's speed. As the pitiless flames arched above it, it bleated a terrified plea the doe could not ignore. She hesitated, turning back for just an instant, to urge her offspring on. The fire caught them together there, consuming both as one, in its ravenous, insatiable hunger.

No life in its path was spared. Rattlesnakes flailed into the air, twisting in momentary agony, then died beside the mice that might have been their meal. Grouse and prairie hens found their wings far too slow to provide escape. Coyote and badger, butterflies and bees, antelope and fox, all were grasped by greedy fingers of fire and fed into the fiery maw of the raging monster of heat and flame.

Hugging low over his horse's neck, Cotton glanced backward again. His horse could not keep up this pace much longer, and even his current pace was painfully inadequate. The fire was gaining on them perceptibly.

Far too long a front to outflank, there was no place to flee. It was only a matter of time until the horse stumbled, or simply tired and slowed, and they would be cremated together.

Unexpectedly, the grass thinned perceptibly beneath his horse's hoofs. For whatever reason, it was more sparse for the distance of twenty yards or so.

Reacting instantly, Cotton fought his terrified horse to a standstill and slid from the saddle. Holding the reins tightly, he fished a match from his pocket. Fighting to hold his plunging, terrified mount and shield the match's small flame at the same time, he ignited a patch of grass. Moving quickly he lit four more small fires.

Almost instantly the wind fanned the small fires into a single flame. It spread swiftly to both sides and forward. Propelled by the wind, it quickly spread beyond the sparser growth, and began to consume the lush supply of fuel the tall, thick grass beyond offered. In minutes it swelled to another massive wall of flame, but this one was moving ahead of and away from them. Small whinnies of terror were emitted from his horse's throat with every breath, as he realized there was now fire both in front of and behind them.

Cotton fought to hold the panicked animal as he lunged and jerked, fighting to free himself to run.

Working feverishly with one hand while he tightly gripped the reins, Cotton unfastened and stripped off his shirt. He rolled it and flipped it around the animal's head, making a blindfold. Instantly the terrified mount's struggles lessened, allowing Cotton to use both hands to tie the blindfold securely into place.

He led the whimpering, quivering animal forward, trotting as fast as he could urge the blindfolded beast, across the newly blackened ground. He followed in the wake of the fire he had set for a little over 200 yards. There, on a patch of ground where the grass had been thinnest, he let the horse stop.

With the speed of stark terror, Cotton ripped his lariat from the saddle. He slipped the loop around the hind leg of his horse, tightening it just above the hoof. Looping the rope over the saddle horn, he hauled the animal's hind leg off the ground at the same time as he jerked hard on the saddle horn.

With no chance to balance himself, the terrified animal fell heavily, landing right in front of his master. Instantly Cotton dallied the rope around the saddle horn, then grabbed his horse's front leg, pulling it upward and tying it to the saddle horn as well.

From behind the cantle he jerked his bedroll and slicker free. He whipped both of them unrolled and spread a blanket across the horse. He spread his slicker over himself and the horse's head, lying down against the terrified beast with his own head just above the animal's.

Reaching across the horse's neck, he gripped the gelding's nose halfway between his nostrils and eyes, holding his head down and still. He talked constantly into the animal's ear.

'Easy, boy. Easy now. It's all right, fella. Just lay easy, boy. Don't kick the blankets off, now,' he crooned.

On and on he droned, sometimes making sense, mostly just making noise, as soothingly as his own surging terror would permit.

The hellish conflagration roared toward them. Its raging bellow rose countless decibels above the roar of a cattle train surrounded by a tornado. It sucked the oxygen from the air and the courage from their hearts in equal measure. It surrounded them, arching above and around them, reaching, stretching to suck them into its monstrous, insatiable maw.

Throat rasping, lungs burning, eyes stinging, Cotton's voice in the darkness beneath the slicker never stopped its croaking cadence of calm in the horse's ear.

Then, as swiftly as it had descended

upon them, the fire was gone, raging east and north to consume a supply of fuel as endless as its appetite, incinerating countless creatures, large and small, along with the tall and brittle grass they had thought would shelter them.

Suddenly something cold and hard pelted against man and animal. It hit them with a hundred tiny stings. Cotton jerked the slicker off of his head, shocked to silence by confusion. Tiny white, round pellets carpeted the blackened ground.

'Hail!' Cotton rasped through a raw throat. Then he laughed, raucously, insanely, falling back upon the ground on his back, arms and legs spread-eagled. He croaked, 'Fire and hail! What next?'

As if in answer the heavens opened. The tiny pellets of hail were replaced with driving, drenching rain, as a summer thunderstorm swept over them.

Cotton struggled to his feet. Head tilted against the onslaught, he released the ropes, allowing his horse to regain his feet. The gelding tossed his head against the blindfold, his nostrils flared still, in fear and confusion. Cotton untied the sleeves of his shirt, pulling it free from the animal's eyes. The horse stood stock-still for a long moment, taking in his blackened surroundings, already soaked by the frigid, driving rain. The air was heavy with the stink of sodden ashes.

Cotton looked toward the fire, racing away from them. It was already hidden from view by the driving rain. He laughed shortly, the sound rasping harshly from his raw throat. 'Ain't that somethin'!' he offered. 'Might even be heavy enough rain to stop that fire. If it don't, there ain't nothin' gonna stop it before it hits the badlands.'

He coiled his rope and secured it to the saddle. He put his soaked shirt back on, blackened as it was from dirt and smoke. He rolled his now sodden blankets and tied them behind the cantle. He stepped into the saddle and began the long ride back through a blackened wasteland. The rain turned into black rivulets, growing into ink-black streams that carried away the remnants of the fire's wake. Skeletons of incinerated animals and occasional rocks were all that broke the sodden blackness of the ground. Washed clean by the rain, they stood as stark memorials to the countless lost lives, large and small. The smell filled his nostrils until he thought he'd be tasting and smelling wet ashes the rest of his life.

'Let's see if we can figure out what started that fire,' he suggested to his now docile horse. 'Or who.'

12

He recognized Grey Wolf, even from this distance. He was flanked by four other Lakota warriors. They sat their horses stolidly, clearly waiting his approach.

'I'll go talk to 'em,' Cotton told Cap.

'Best take a couple of us along,' Cap advised.

Cotton shook his head. 'That lance he's showin' means he wants to talk, not fight.'

'You trust 'im?'

Cotton hesitated a long moment. 'Yeah, I do. I couldn't tell you why. I only talked to him once. But I think he's a man of his word. I think I trust him.'

'He's an Indian.'

Cotton shrugged. 'An honest one, if I'm any judge o' people.'

'Your funeral.' Cap shrugged in

obvious disagreement.

Ignoring him, Cotton nudged his horse to a trot toward the waiting five. He rode directly to Grey Wolf, reining in ten feet from him. The two looked at each other in silence for several heartbeats. It was Grey Wolf who spoke first, in his surprisingly good English. 'Your hair is shorter than the last time I saw you.'

Cotton grinned. 'Yeah, the ends sorta got singed off.'

Grey Wolf's expression did not change, but his eyes twinkled. 'It is a strange way to have your hair made shorter.'

'Strange way to roast a horse, too, but I came pretty close to doin' that too.'

'Roast horse is good meat.'

Cotton shook his head. 'I'd a lot rather ride 'im than eat 'im.'

Grey Wolf's eyes were suddenly serious. 'My people will be eating our horses to keep the winter from being a dying time,' he said.

'Bad year?' Cotton enquired, even

though he already knew the answer.

'The buffalo still have not come. It is late in the year. They should be here now, but they have not come. Instead you have come, with many cattle that eat the grass the buffalo would come for. Now you have even burned the grass your cattle have not eaten.'

Cotton shook his head. 'It sure wasn't us that started that fire! As a matter of fact, as I 'spect you already know, I was smack in the path of it. If I hadn't set a new fire and tied my horse down on burnt ground, it'd have roasted us both alive. I figured out where it started, but it'd rained so hard there weren't any tracks left, so I couldn't tell who started it.'

Again, Grey Wolf stared at him a long time before responding. 'I saw your tracks that came back from where the fire passed over you. The fire was made for you. It is rare that one would escape such a fire.'

'It was set for me?'

'It was one of your men who made it.

He watched you, then made the fire. He knew such tall grass and fast wind would make too big a fire to run away from, so it would kill you.'

'You watched him set the fire?'

'He was seen,' Grey Wolf evaded.

'One of my own hands did it?'

The Indian's silence confirmed it. 'What one?' Cotton demanded.

Grey Wolf simply shook his head, refusing to answer.

It wasn't as if Cotton needed to have the offender identified. At the same time as the fire occurred, Hank Houston had disappeared. He had already cursed himself a dozen times for not pressing the Texan, after Timmy had revealed the man's intent to kill him during the Arapaho attack.

Rather than answer the needless question, Grey Wolf pursued his own purpose. 'You drive many cattle through Lakota land. They eat the grass the buffalo should come for. You burn the grass you do not eat. We must have cattle to pay for letting you pass through the land of the Lakota.'

Cotton pondered the demand in silence. Grey Wolf had already made it clear the Lakota would not attack his outfit head on. They had learned from the disaster the Arapaho suffered, the futility of that tactic. But they could launch forays against the edges of the herd, against the remuda, even against the wagons in small raids that would exact a toll too great to be acceptable. He knew there was a time to stand firm and tough. He knew, as well, that there were times when it was better to find an alternative to a deadly, and probably unwinnable, confrontation. It would be far better if he could bargain his way through this one.

With his face as impassive as that of the Indian, he asked, 'How many cattle does Grey Wolf believe would be a fair price, just to pass through Lakota land, eating only so very small a portion of such plentiful grass?'

The immediacy of the answer revealed the question had already been well discussed amongst themselves. 'One hundred cows. Two good bulls. Enough for food now and for the winter, and enough to have calves of our own for other winters.'

Mentally tallying numbers, Cotton reckoned the price to be tolerable. He also knew it was a first demand, and he would lose all respect of the Lakota if he did not argue the price at length. As if they were casually discussing weather, Cotton responded, 'That's an awful lot of cows. Too many. It would be a reasonable price, I 'spect, if you were to ask for ten cows. Throwing in a bull would make it kinda steep. But I reckon as how we could maybe offer you ten cows and one bull.'

'It is not so small a thing to bring so many cattle through the land of the Lakota,' Grey Wolf responded.

'But they are our cattle,' Cotton argued, 'and there is much grass this year. They eat only a little of it.'

The conversation went on for more than an hour. In the end, Grey Wolf agreed to a 'toll' of thirty-five cows and one bull.

'You must keep your young men from killing the bull for sport,' Cotton cautioned. 'If they do, and the cows you have left are bred by a buffalo, their calves will be too big. The cows will die giving birth.'

Grey Wolf studied his face a long moment. 'It has been done?' he asked. 'To breed cattle and buffalo together?'

Cotton nodded. 'It's been done some. I am told it doesn't work too bad, if your bull breeds buffalo cows. Their calves are strong, and the cows have them without problems. But buffalo bulls are too big and heavy. Sometimes they harm the cow's back or legs with their weight, when they breed. And their calves are always too big for the cows to give birth without help. If you can haze a few stray buffalo heifers away from the herd and keep them with your cows, though, you can have a lot of cattle from one bull.'

His face not betraying the direction of his thoughts, Grey Wolf remained silent a long moment. 'It is a good thing to think about,' he said eventually.

He waved his hand toward the tips of a distant stand of trees to the east. 'My young men will wait at those trees for the cows and the good, young bull you have promised.'

Cotton smiled tightly at the emphasis Grey Wolf put on the 'young' description of the bull. That had not been mentioned before. He knew that, by agreeing, it would become a binding part of the agreement. It seemed fair. He nodded, turned his horse wordlessly, and trotted back to the waiting wagons.

Chet Holland and Cap were waiting for him at the edge of the wagons. 'That powwow took long enough! What's the deal?' Chet called as Cotton drew within earshot.

Cotton held his answer until he reined in next to the pair. He looped his right leg around the saddle horn, resting his back and legs. 'They asked for a hundred cows and two young bulls as a toll for goin' through their

148

land,' he announced.

Chet studied his face for signs he wasn't being toyed with. 'Kinda steep, ain't it?'

Cotton nodded. 'They never expected to get their first demand. I did think it'd be better to pay 'em off than have 'em nippin' at the edges o' the herd all the way through their land. I agreed to thirty cows and one young bull. Made 'im promise they'd use the bull for breedin', an' eat the calves, instead o' just killin' 'em all right away.'

'Do you think they will?'

Cotton's eyes were distant. 'Hard to say. Normally, I'd say no. But Grey Wolf has got a good head on 'im. I told 'im how they could work some buffalo heifers into the herd and cross-breed, and build up a herd of their own, so they wouldn't have to depend on the buffalo gettin' here on time every year. I think he's givin' it serious thought.'

Chet's voice was dry as he said, 'I don't s'pose you figgered on any o' them thirty head o' cows bein' your stock.'

Cotton grinned. 'As a matter o' fact, I did. I figured ten of 'em oughta be mine.'

Chet's eyebrows went up, obviously impressed. 'That's fair enough. Cap, have a couple o' the boys cut out thirty head o' cows. Have 'em keep their calves with 'em. That'll give 'em somethin' to kill an' eat right away, without cuttin' down on next year's calf crop, if there is one. Oh, an' cut out that ringy little part-Brahma bull to go with 'em. He's feisty enough to rustle feed through the winter, an' maybe even teach 'em a thing or two about handlin' cattle.'

Three hours later the cattle had been separated and delivered. The hands that delivered them returned with a message for Cotton. 'Grey Wolf said to tell you he's impressed with your honor, because you left the calves with the cows. He said to tell you that Grey Wolf is your brother, whatever that means.'

Nearly overcome suddenly with an emotion he little understood and even less expected, Cotton only nodded, wheeled his horse and rode away.

13

'We shoulda hugged closer to the Black Hills.'

Cotton frowned in response. 'I shoulda scouted further ahead, anyway,' he conceded. 'When Tim told me about this stretch o' country, I thought he was exaggeratin'.'

Cap Lindiken nodded. 'It didn't make any more sense to me than it did to you.'

'It seemed like a good idea to stay a ways away from the Black Hills if we could. The Lakota get pretty touchy about that area.'

'I've heard rumors they's gold layin' plumb on top o' the ground, in them hills.'

'I've heard that. I've also heard about a lot of guys that tried sneakin' in to see if they could nab onto some of it, too. They have a strange way o' never bein' heard from again.'

Cap nodded in grudging agreement.

'I've known half a dozen men who headed there. I ain't never seen a one of 'em again.'

'This can't be any better to try to get through, though,' Cotton lamented, looking ahead at the strange land.

In the distant west, the top of the Black Hills was barely visible. Between there and where he sat his horse, there was no tree in sight. Instead the hills were covered with tall grass, and lay in wrinkled and buckled chaos.

From where he sat, the ground fell away into a deep canyon, with moderately steep sides. It was easily navigable by horse. Cattle had no trouble traversing it. But the wagons were another matter entirely. The sides of the canyons were so steep that even tripling the size of the teams barely made them able to ascend. Compounding the problem, the canyons led nowhere.

'I've never seen country that the lie of the land didn't go one general direction,' Cotton puzzled. 'Even in them endless sandhills, down in Nebraska, the draws pertneart always run east and west. And they went somewheres. They always headed downhill to where they'd eventually find a river. This country makes no sense at all.'

As he said, there was no pattern to the land whatever. Canyons led in every direction imaginable. They lay, sometimes, at right angles to one another, without being connected. To travel from one to another, it was necessary to climb to the top of the ridge, either at its end or a side. From there the land fell away into another canyon, which went a different direction altogether.

It was as if the entire area were a large piece of cloth that simply became randomly wrinkled, the folds leading no place, the ridges twisted and tumbled haphazardly.

Most of the canyons were at least half a mile wide. Many were wider. Some of them, if they were followed far enough, led to a high ridge that blocked the canyon completely. If there were sufficient rainfall, the water would simply be trapped in that canyon, to form a permanent lake or evaporate.

That such canyons were not filled with water attested to the paucity of rainfall. Only until late spring was there any standing water, most years.

To say the least, it was a complete nightmare to try to move a wagon train and herd of cattle through it. On cloudy or overcast days it was even impossible to maintain a sense of direction. On the second consecutive overcast day, the lead wagon cut across the trail they had made the day before.

Chet Holland spared no words in confronting Cotton. 'I thought you had scouts out, Lang,' he accused. 'We ain't doin' nothin' but stumblin' around like blind men in a root cellar with the door closed. We're just gettin' more lost every time we cross the same ridge.'

Cotton tried in vain to think of an answer that would vindicate his leadership. None came to mind. He merely shrugged instead. 'Dangdest country I've ever seen.' The answer sounded lame, even to him.

'Well, you best get your hindside in gear and find us a way out've it, is all I got to say,' the herd owner ordered.

He wheeled his horse and rode away, to Cotton's relief.

He turned and looked back at the following herd, far more worried than he wanted Chet to know. If they didn't find their way out of the maze they'd wandered into, the cattle would quickly grow desperate for water. There was a limit to how long the mules could haul wagons up and down those canyon sides, as well.

The last thing he needed was one more worry to cloud his mind. As seems to be the way with life, he was given that one more within the hour.

From the direction of the herd, a lone rider topped a ridge and dropped out of sight into the intervening canyon. Cotton frowned, failing to recognize him or the horse he was riding. He turned, waiting for the man to emerge from the canyon.

He did so, within half an hour. He rode directly to Cotton. 'Cotton Lang?' he called out as he approached.

Cotton nodded. 'Last I knew, that was me,' he responded.

'Well, you don't look too dead,' the rider observed.

'Am I supposed to be?'

'Yup. That's the word. Dead as a doornail and burned to a cinder.'

'Is that so? And how did I get to be so dead?'

'Why, didn't you know? You got caught in one God-awful prairie fire and couldn't get away. Burned you up so bad they couldn't even pick up what was left of your body. Just buried the charred bones as best they could, right along with the bones of the horse you was ridin'.'

Half a dozen things raced through Cotton's mind. Instead of giving voice to any of them, he said, 'Who're you?'

The rider grinned. 'Name's Tad Willington.'

'Never heard of you.'

'Didn't figger you had. I hired onto the Double O Bar a couple weeks after ya'll left.'

'Come up from Texas with a trail herd?' Cotton guessed.

'Yup. My first one. Last one, too. That ain't no life for me.'

'So what are you doing way up here?'

'Chasin' after you, up until just now.'

'Why?'

'Cuz your woman didn't believe what she was bein' told. She said if 'n y'all was dead, she'da felt it in 'er bones. She figgered she was bein' fed a string o' lies. She was some shook up, though. So me, bein' a fine an' true gentleman an' all, offered to catch up to your herd an' find out if 'n y'all was dead or alive.'

Cotton digested the gush of information, fighting down a surge of anger at the levity of the dancing-eyed cowboy. His words were harsher than he intended. 'How about you stop bein' funny and start at the beginning, and tell me the whole story.'

The cowboy's eyes instantly grew

more serious. 'Sorry. Didn't mean to be makin' light o' things. Just plumb tickled to see y'all lookin' all fit an' fuzzy.'

Cotton waited in silence. Willington took a deep breath. 'I 'spect it must've been three weeks ago, give or take, one o' your drovers come ridin' back to Ogallala.'

'Hank Houston,' Cotton guessed.

Tad nodded in agreement. 'Yeah. That's what his name was. He come back tellin' a story 'bout this fearsome prairie fire that went sweepin' through the country. That was some fire! I rode around the edge o' where it burnt. Couldn't see the other side. Rode far enough into it to see it'd killed everything in its path. I seen a bunch o' antelope bones, even. I thought an antelope could outrun anything!'

'You're driftin' some from the story.'

'Yeah. Sorry. Anyway, this guy comes back with this story about you bein' burned to a crisp in that fire, so you ain't comin' back for your woman.

159

There's this other guy that sure wants that woman, an' he's startin' to move right in, tellin' 'er it's her destiny to marry him.'

'Dugger,' Cotton grunted.

'That's the fella! But Miss Owens, she ain't buyin' it for a minute. But she don't know how she's gonna find out. Now me, I been on this trail drive, an' I know how slow them steers move, so I figger cows an' calves gotta move even slower. Not to mention them big wagons. So I told that there little ol' girl o' yours that I could ride up here an' catch up with you, find out what the truth is, an' hightail it right back there. I can be caught up to y'all an' back again in two or three weeks, I tell her. So she got jist plumb tickled an' asked me if'n I'd do that. So here I am. I figgered at the very worst, my bein' willin' to do that, an' all, would pertneart guarantee me a job with her ol' man.'

Cotton nodded. His visage betrayed nothing of the roiling emotions within.

160

Everything in his being strained to ride out immediately, to take vengeance on Houston, and on Dugger, who he was certain had hired Houston, and claim his bride.

But he was a man of honour and integrity. He had promised to see a herd to Montana Territory. They were still almost a month away from their goal. To leave now would place the entire herd in jeopardy.

To leave with them floundering in this maze of senseless canyons and ridges would only compound that jeopardy.

His voice steady, he said, 'Well, you'd best stay the night. Get some rest. Take a fresh horse, and head back as quick as you can. Tell Esther I'm fine, and I'll be after her in about a month and a half.'

'You want me to pass the word that Hank Houston is a liar, while I'm at it?'

Cotton had already noted the well-worn six-shooter on the young man's hip. It was obvious he was itching for an excuse to back Houston against a wall.

But Cotton wanted that satisfaction for himself. He shook his head. 'Houston's mine. So's Dugger. Just look after Esther.'

Tad grinned. 'Oh, you don't need me for that! That young fella you give that job is doin' just fine.'

'Thirsty?'

'That's the boy. He's just plumb made a full-time job outa keepin' an eye on her for ya. Even that Dugger fella can't get near 'er without Thirsty just happenin' to be right there handy. I ain't sure how long that's gonna last, though.'

'Why's that?'

Tad shrugged. 'Seems just a matter o' time till some unfortunate accident's gonna happen to that boy. He's irritatin' the wrong people. Dugger or his boys, either one'll put a chunk o' lead into 'im outa the dark some-wheres.'

'Thirsty's better at takin' care of himself than he acts,' Cotton argued.

Tad shrugged again. 'Maybe. Even

so, the most careful of us can get surprised. It only takes one hunk o' lead outa the dark.'

The young Texan was one day away from bearing his good news to Esther when his words became eerily prescient. He never even felt the piece of lead hurtling from the darkness, that ripped his own life away, leaving his lifeless body lying beside his confused horse. The message he bore with his customary bubbling exuberance died with him, unheard by its intended recipient.

14

The Indian was a welcome sight. That, in itself, said a lot about Cotton's state of mind.

They had floundered nearly a week within the twisted canyons and senseless patterns of the broken grassland. He was no nearer than when they entered to finding a way out that both cattle and wagons could navigate.

Grey Wolf appeared in front of him, as if by magic, just after sunup. He jumped so hard he startled his own horse.

Grey Wolf's face didn't acknowledge Cotton's surprise, but his eyes reflected the pleasure at being able to startle him. 'My brother wanders aimlessly,' he announced, rather than asked.

Cotton nodded, making no effort to pretend to be anything but lost in the vast array of confusing canyons. 'This country doesn't make any sense to me,' he admitted.

Grey Wolf nodded. 'It is something, I think, that The Great Spirit tossed out. Perhaps, like an old blanket, it was land He had no use for, so He cast it aside, and let it settle to the earth by itself, wrinkled, as it fell. Or perhaps He made it this way on purpose, to confuse those who grow too proud.'

'Well, I didn't think I was too proud, but He's sure enough got me confused.'

'My brother will lose his cattle wandering among these waterless canyons.'

'That's what I'm afraid of.'

'Why did you not stay closer to the mountains, where the land lies as a land ought to lie?'

'I didn't want to crowd into country sacred to your people,' Cotton acknowledged. 'I thought we could stay far enough away you'd know we respected that.'

Grey Wolf grunted noncommitally. After several minutes, he said simply, 'Follow.'

He turned his horse, heading down toward the bottom of the canyon. Silently Cotton followed, as he was bidden.

In the canyon bottom, Grey Wolf turned left, nudging his horse to a quick trot. As it appeared the canyon would dead-end in a tall ridge, the Indian turned right around a small hogback. He rode up over a gentle rise, which opened, surprisingly, down into an even wider, flatter canyon. He turned right in it, seeming to Cotton as if they were reversing directions completely.

They continued that way, taking unexpected turns into canyons that were easier to traverse than any he had yet found. By mid-afternoon, they had emerged onto a high plateau that sloped gently downward to the west. In the distance Cotton could see the crooked line of trees that marked the Cheyenne River. Grey Wolf lifted his arm, pointing. 'When you are there, where it is flat, you can again turn north. Keep the Paha Sapa half a day on your left hand, and the way will be easy. When you get to the edge of the country of the Crow, you will find the rivers you seek, where there are already people and two towns. It will be good to have my brother between our land and that of the Crow.'

Cotton stood in his stirrups, studying out the land that lay before him. It appeared to be exactly as Grey Wolf had said. From the flat land he could see in the distance, he was sure they would be able to spot Buffalo Gap. From there, it would be just a matter of putting days together, one on top of the other, until they arrived at their destination.

Jubilant, after a week of increasing confusion and despondency, he turned to thank the Lakota. There was no trace of him.

Cotton's head jerked this way and that, straining to catch a glimpse of the Indian, to know in what direction he had gone, how he had disappeared so quickly. He saw nothing.

As he backtracked to the wagons and the herd he marveled at how seldom he could even see a trace of the Lakota's passing. His own horse had left an easy trail for his keen and carefully trained eye to follow. Even it, however, found only occasional traces of Grey Wolf. He was grateful for even those faint traces. In his present state of mind, he wouldn't have been sure whether the Indian's presence had been real or some apparition, without those traces of assurance.

It was nearly sunset when he rode into the circle of wagons, camped in the bottom of a canyon in which they had found water. He had kept the herd where it was, sending six scouts out to try to find a way out of the maze he had gotten them mazed in. He was the first to return.

'Find anything?' Chet Holland demanded, even as his boot touched the ground.

Cotton nodded, accepting gratefully the steaming cup of coffee Ramona McGhghy handed him. 'I know the way out,' he announced. 'It's tricky, but not a hard drive. It'll only take us one long day to be out of the canyons. Another short day'll put us over to the Cheyenne River. From there we can go through Buffalo Gap, then follow along the east side of the Black Hills.'

Holland peered hard at him. 'You're sure, this time?'

Cotton nodded, trying not to bristle at the challenge. 'Had some help,' he admitted. 'Them cows an' the bull we gave the Indians just paid off big time. Grey Wolf showed up. He showed me the way out.'

Suspicion clouded Holland's eyes. 'And you trust him?'

A murmur among those who had assembled to listen echoed the rancher's attitude. Cotton chose to ignore it. He simply nodded. 'I trust him. Not to mention, I rode all the way to where I could see the river with him, then followed my own tracks back again. I gotta admit, though, I don't think I'd have ever figured out the way without him. Even with him, it seemed like we were just doubling back again and again. Then, all of a sudden, we were out of the canyons.'

After a long pause, Holland said, 'One day, huh?'

Cotton nodded again. 'Might be a long day, but we can do it in a day. We'll leave at first light.'

'The others aren't back yet,' Holland protested.

'None of 'em?'

'None of 'em. Wouldn't be surprised if they're all as lost as we been. We may never see 'em again.'

Cotton thought about it for quite a bit. He looked around carefully. In one direction from where they were camped there was an exceptionally high ridge. Studying it, he nodded. 'It'll be a full moon tonight. They can see to ride, if they know what direction to go. I'll have a big fire built up on top of that ridge. Keep it burnin' all night. They'll be able to see it from wherever they've wandered.'

'Beacon fire,' Holland muttered. 'Draw the Indians right to us.'

'They already know where we're at,' Cotton reminded him. 'It's our own boys who need to know where we are.'

It was a brilliant solution. Even so, it was only a couple hours short of daybreak when the last of the scouts were guided back to camp by the fire's light.

They were little more than settled into their bedrolls when Cotton was ringing the cook's bell. Everyone, however, rolled out of bed instantly with the first clanging of the wake-up call. The morning was electric with hope and anticipation. The teams were harnessed, wagons moving, herd gathered and started, with the remuda bringing up the rear, in less time than any morning since they had left Ogallala. Even the animals seemed to sense the prospect of finally escaping the clutches of the endless, convoluted canyons.

Pressing harder and longer than any

day of the drive, they could not make themselves stop until they had descended the last, long hill, into the bottom-land. They camped that night along the waters of the Cheyenne River.

Cotton, quite by accident, found a hot spring that emptied into the river. After thinking about it, he passed the word of its presence to the grateful women in the wagons. Its waters provided the first hot bath any of them had had since leaving home.

The last of the campfires had died to glowing embers when his ebullient sense of well-being came crashing down once again.

First one, then several of the dogs in camp began to bark a warning. Then one of the sentries appeared among the wagons, with a stranger in tow. 'Man lookin' for Cotton,' the sentry announced.

'Right here,' Cotton said, even as he felt the rising tingle of apprehension.

'Cotton Lang?' the newcomer asked again.

'That's me.'

'In the flesh?'

'I sure seem to be. Who're you?'

'Name's Buster Flagg. I ride for Double O Bar.'

The apprehension in Cotton escalated markedly. 'What's wrong?'

The man hesitated a couple heartbeats. 'Don't know how to say it easy. It's about your friend, Thirsty.'

'Thirsty Williams?'

The man nodded. 'He's been shot.'

Silence overwhelmed the group that had assembled around them as if by magic. Cotton's voice was as flat and empty as fleeting hope. 'Dead?' he demanded.

Again the man nodded. 'Never knew what hit 'im.'

'Who?'

'No idea. Happened just afore dark. He was standin' in the yard, just outside the corral. Rifleman in the trees east o' the yard shot 'im in the back. Right between the shoulders. Dead afore he hit the ground.'

'Are Esther and her family all right?'

It seemed as if the man's head wasn't going to stop its bobbing nod all night. 'They're fine. Nothin' happened at all after Thirsty was shot. They wanted me to catch up to the herd and tell you. Well, that, an' to find out if you was still alive.'

Alarms sounded instantly in Cotton's mind. 'They don't know? Didn't she get my message?'

The man swallowed hard before he shook his head. 'That there's the other thing I gotta tell you. I'm sorry. Tad never made it back. I know he made it here, 'cause I found the horse with his saddle an' stuff. He was a friend o' mine. I backtracked the horse. He was shot the same way. Outa the trees. Pertneart a day's ride north o' the place. Never had a chance.'

Dark tendrils of despair stretched across Cotton's mind, threatening to engulf him, to smother him, to snuff out all the joyous hopes and plans for his and Esther's future. Guilt followed hard on the despair, condemning him for not marrying her before he left, bringing her along with the other women, keeping her where he could protect her. He knew with sudden certainty the he couldn't even get word to her, to tell her he was still alive. How could he expect her to wait for him, if she were continually told he was dead?

At the same time, how could he go to her, walking away from the responsibility for all these other lives? Their hopes, their future, their very lives depended on his fulfilling his promise to get them and the herd to their destination. He was trapped, locked in an unresolvable dilemma.

His desperation and despair must have shown in his eyes, even in the lesser light of the full moon. Buster said, 'Don't worry. I'll get word back to her.'

Ineffable sadness gave a hollow echo to his words. 'They'll just kill you before you can get there, just like they did Thirsty and Tad.'

Buster grinned unexpectedly. 'Only if they know what direction I'm comin' from.'

A faint glimmer of hope sprang up on the horizon of Cotton's mind. He reached for it instantly. 'You think there's a way you can make it?'

'Count on it,' Buster affirmed. 'I can be slicker'n badger grease on a wagon wheel when I need to be. They won't even know I'm on the way till I step off the train in Ogallala. And by then I'll already have a telegram sent with the message anyway.'

Cotton mulled it over carefully in his mind. From what Buster had said, he knew exactly what the man had planned. In his mind he followed the circuitous route that would bring him to the railroad miles east of Ogallala. The train would be the last place in the world they would expect his return. It just might work! He grinned just as unexpectedly as the messenger had. 'Then do it. And tell Esther not to let on, though. And keep your own head down. It'll be another month before I show up. I wouldn't want anyone gettin' jittery an' quittin' the country afore I have a chance to say 'Howdy'.'

Buster glanced up at the sky. 'I've got another four hours o' good moonlight. If I can bum a good horse in trade for this wore-out one, I'll head back right now.'

In answer, Cotton simply extended his hand. Buster took it in a grip of new friendship that both knew was a bond meant to last.

15

'That's Buffalo Gap, yonder.'

Cotton nodded. He swiped his sleeve across his brow, wiping away the sweat. The move left a streak of clean skin across his forehead. The rest of his face and clothing was covered with red dust. 'I recognized it. Herd's strung out straight for it. We oughta be across it by night.'

'Best not,' Cap Lindiken disagreed.

'Why not? It's about the right distance.'

'You ain't seen that dust yonder?' Cap pointed.

'Hadn't noticed it,' Cotton admitted. 'What do you suppose it is?'

'Buffalo. They're later'n usual, but they're migratin' north. They'll be headin' for the gap too.'

Cotton pursed his lips. 'Well, we sure don't wanta be fightin' them for who gets to go first,' he observed.

Cap grunted his agreement. ''Specially goin' through the gap. From here it looks like a saddle in the hills. It's pretty wide, when you get in it. But when a herd o' buffalo is headin' through it, it's plumb filled up. They'd either stampede our herd or trample 'em to death. Them buffalo is big animals.'

'We ought to get one for the camp.'

'Be a change o' diet,' Cap agreed. 'I doubt if most of 'em has ever et buffalo.'

'Me either,' Cotton admitted. 'I hear it's good.'

'Fine meat,' Cap confirmed. 'It's a bit grainier than beef. Not as much fat. Get a fat yearlin' though, and everybody'll enjoy it.'

'Let's do it,' Cotton decided.

They rode toward a point where they could easily intersect the moving cloud of dust that indicated the buffaloes' presence. As they drew nearer, other sounds intruded.

Cap's voice lost its casual tone instantly. 'Best find some cover,' he said, already moving for a brush filled gully.

By the time they reached the gully the sounds were growing louder. They tethered their horses in thick brush in the bottom of the gulch, then crawled to the top. Watching through low sage that effectively masked their presence, they watched an incredible scene unfold before them.

A herd of tens of thousands of buffalo were running. The ground shook and trembled with the pounding of the thousands of hoofs. Dust rose in clouds.

Adding to the din was the yells and whoops of dozens of Indians, riding fearlessly on the fringes of the thundering herd. Most had rifles, though some still clung to their traditional bows and arrows. As each was able to ride close beside a running buffalo, they shot, nearly point blank, into the neck, or behind the front leg of the huge beast.

Even shot at point blank range, the animal would continue on for a surprisingly long way before collapsing from internal hemorrhaging. Even before that one fell, the hunter was furiously kicking his horse in pursuit of the next.

It took half an hour for the seemingly numberless herd to thunder its way past, taking with it the whooping, hollering hunters. In their wake the low hills were spotted with dead buffalo.

Following behind the hunters, Indian women and children descended on the dead animals. Working furiously, there was almost no talk between them. Every ounce of their energy was devoted to conserving and utilizing the results of the hunt. Their survival through the following winter depended on how well they did their work.

They skinned and gutted the huge carcasses with uncanny efficiency. They carefully removed stomachs and bladders to be used as water bags. They sliced off pieces of liver to eat raw, as they worked, to maintain their energy and strength. They cut the animals into pieces they could lift, and either carried them away or loaded them, along with the heavy hides, onto horses or crudely fashioned travois, for transport back to their village.

Even before they finished, coyotes and wolves, eagles, buzzards, magpies, and dozens of lesser birds and animals were swarming toward the scene of the slaughter, anticipating their own feast on the easy abundance of food.

Later, when the people had all gone, mountain lions, lynx, bobcats, even badgers and countless rodents would take advantage of the bounty. In days the gut piles would be gone, the bones picked bare to bleach in the sun.

'We'd best ease outa here,' Cap whispered.

They worked their way silently back below the crest of the hill. Hurrying as swiftly as silence permitted, they returned to their horses and worked their way along the bottom of the gully. When it flattened out enough to permit, they struck off at right angles, heading back toward their own herd and the wagons that accompanied it.

'Well, so much for gettin' a buffalo,' Cotton lamented.

'Just keep your eyes peeled,' Cap disagreed. 'There'll be some that broke off from the herd. We'll ride onto some. We're far enough away from the Indians now they won't even notice an extra shot or two.'

'You think so?'

'Sure,' Cap said, dismissing Cotton's misgivings with his tone. 'Not only that, but the Indians ain't likely to notice the dust of our herd, goin' through the gap. They'll think it's just another bunch o' buffalo, and they already got all the buffalo their women can take care of for several weeks. They'll eat themselves sleepy and swap lies about the hunt till we're plumb out of their territory.'

'Well, that'll save having to peel off another bunch of cows to avoid a fight,' Cotton appreciated.

As if to make his words prophetic,

the next rise they topped revealed half a dozen young buffalo, nervously cropping grass in the bottom of a swale.

They reined in, studying the huge animals. 'If they hadn't been run already, we could ride up pertneart to 'em,' Cap said. 'But they'll be a bit skittish. They're workin' their way up thataway. If we slip around and lie low just past that little hogback runnin' out there, we oughta be in good position for a shot.'

Cotton nodded, following the older man's lead.

They again tethered their horses, well out of sight or sound of the presumed path the buffalo would follow. Then they positioned themselves, lying flat in the tall grass, just past the rise of ground. Less than a hundred feet in front of them, the point of ground tapered off to the flat bottom, where the grass was still as lush and green as if it were late spring.

They waited less than twenty minutes before the first buffalo emerged. Head down, oblivious to everything, a year-ling bull walked along slowly, tearing and munching great mouthfuls of the succulent grass. Behind him the others followed.

His voice barely audible to the man beside him, Cap whispered, 'Let's take the lead bull. Right behind the front leg. Both together. Ready?'

'Yeah,' Cotton breathed.

Surprised at the hammering of his heart, Cotton cocked his rifle, aiming along the barrel at the great animal. Cap's rifle roared beside him. Instinctively, his own finger twitched the trigger in instant response, the discharge of his own rifle so instantly behind that of Cap's that the two shots blurred into one.

The buffalo grunted and jerked his head up in surprise. Those behind him wheeled and plunged away, then slowed when they saw no reason for their sudden panic.

The one they had shot spun around, his front feet planted, his lighter back quarters doing the moving. Then he spun back again, looking for the source of the sudden noise, and his own increasing discomfort. He shook his massive head, as if confused by something he failed to understand. He took an uncharacteristic step backward, then a step sideways. He toppled over, into the tall grass, dead before he hit the ground.

Cotton stared in awe. 'Two slugs that size in the heart, from that range, and it took him that long to go down!' he marveled.

Cap nodded as he stood. 'If we'da jumped up an' spooked him as soon as we shot, he'd still be runnin',' he said.

As they stood, the others in the small bunch spooked for the first time. They thundered off, back the way they had come.

They walked to the downed animal. Laying his rifle aside, Cotton grasped the animal's horns. He strained to lift just the animal's head clear of the ground. 'This thing is huge!'

'Aw, it's only a yearlin'. He's only about half growed. Think how hard he'd be to take care of, if he was full growed.'

'How in the world do those Indian women handle these things?' he marveled.

'They're tougher'n whang leather, that's for sure,' Cap agreed. 'Too bad we ain't got our women trained to do the same.'

He turned, as if speaking to an imaginary woman. 'Here, woman, I done shot the critter, now you get it skinned an' gutted, an' you take care o' the meat an' stuff. Get it all cut into thin strips so you can smoke it and jerk it and whatever you want to do with it, so's it'll be good for winter. And then you can get the hide stretched and staked and scraped so you can tan it later. I'm plumb awful tired from all that shootin'. I'm gonna take a nap.'

Cotton chuckled. 'We could use some help,' he offered. 'The wagons are less than a mile over. One of us can get to work skinnin' this thing, and the other could ride to the wagons and get some others to help get it dressed out.'

'You skin, I'll ride,' Cap grinned.

'Fair enough,' Cotton agreed, already struggling to get his razor-sharp knife through the thick hide of the enormous animal.

The animal would not only provide a change of diet. It would provide the meat for the whole outfit for as long as they could keep it from spoiling.

16

The knot in his stomach would not go away. Each time he lifted the reins, willed his spurs to touch the gray gelding's side, to move forward, something stopped him. Each time, as soon as he stopped, a cold chill spread through him, as if he had just escaped some great danger.

He could not explain the feeling. Neither could he argue with it. It held him riveted where he was, screened from view, unable to proceed.

Cotton sat his horse in the edge of a thick stand of timber. Before him lay a broad sweep of open land, falling away gently to the Dismal River. 'Not much of a river, but it sure looks dismal all right,' Cotton muttered under his breath.

There was no way forward from here without crossing a great breadth of open ground. Beyond the Dismal, the Sand Hills provided decent cover, though treeless. Their folds and creases made hundreds of options for a man on horseback to keep to low ground. He could easily avoid the eyes of any watcher, barring a freak chance encounter. Such an encounter would surprise the other every bit as much as him, giving him an even chance of having the quicker reflexes.

This spot, however, was tailor-made for an ambush. The broad sweep of land had no place to cross with any measure of cover whatever.

He momentarily second-guessed himself on choice of routes. He could have spent an extra day riding, chosen a random, looping path, and made it all but impossible for anyone to lie in wait for him to ride past.

He could not force himself to take that extra day. The knot in his gut told him he might already be too late.

He had worked as fast as he was able, once the herd was finally at its destination. Cotton's cattle, as well as those of three of Chet Holland's neighbors who had accompanied them, were cut out from Holland's stock. Cap Lindiken kept his stock with Cotton's, having agreed to be Cotton's foreman, and to run his own stock on the same land with Cotton's.

When the herds were all separated, each was driven to the land their owner claimed, to begin the process of building a ranch. Logs were already being cut, trimmed, and dragged, to erect cabins. Those cabins would see their families through the harsh Montana winter. Next spring they would be expanded into roomier houses, and barns and corrals would join them. There was talk around the area that a group of Norwegians planned to build a sawmill, which would provide cut lumber by spring. For now, though, the need was constructing quick shelter. A covered wagon would be a miserable place for a family to spend a winter.

As soon as he possibly could, Cotton

left. He rode his big iron-gray gelding, and brought along a stout pinto mare on a lead rope. That allowed him to switch back and forth between the horses, tiring them less quickly.

Some small voice within him kept up an incessant goading to hurry, hurry, hurry. He didn't know if it stemmed from his intense longing for Esther, or from some mystical premonition of danger confronting her. It might well have been both.

He had made extremely quick time on his road south. Each horse, as it was led, quickly learned to hurry as far ahead as the lead rope allowed, then grab a couple mouthfuls of grass before the tether forced it to catch up again. In that manner, the led horse was able to ingest considerable nourishment, even while on the move.

He rode at a ground-eating trot, eyes roving the horizon and all possible places of cover. Those restless eyes never stopped searching, seeking, probing, watching for an ambush he was certain would come, sooner or later.

There was no better spot within a hundred miles for it to come. The cliff skirting the north side of the river offered few spots feasible for descent. The broadest of those, through which they had driven the northward bound herd, lay just in front of him.

'Gotta be six hundred yards wide,' he reasoned with the gray gelding. 'If I stay pretty well to center, if somebody's holed up on either side, he'll have close to a three-hundred-yard shot.'

Even as he said it, he knew that wasn't nearly enough.

'If I circle to the closest way down to either side, it'll cost me half a day,' he continued to explain to the patient animal. 'And both of them spots is narrow enough a man in hidin' pertneart couldn't miss.'

The gelding grew tired of the discussion, shaking his head impatiently at the long delay. 'All right, all right,' Cotton muttered. 'I ain't waitin' ten more hours till dark. Let's push it, and see what happens.'

He left the cover of the trees at a swift trot. Fifty yards from the trees, he veered to his right. It would appear to anyone watching that he was heading for the western edge of the break in the cliff.

Fifty yards further on he veered back, cutting an oblique angle toward the other extreme of the gentler slope leading south.

He rode a good hundred yards in that direction before veering back the other way once again. 'Lot of wasted time if there's one on each side,' he remonstrated against himself.

Even so, he continued the tactic until the ground began to drop significantly. There was no sign of any danger. Nothing marred the tranquility of the autumn morning. He began to relax. The knot in his stomach eased, ever so little.

Suddenly a crow rose from a clump of trees 200 yards ahead of him, cawing loudly. Without any conscious thought,

Cotton flopped forward onto the gelding's neck. His spurs jammed into the animal's sides. He dropped the pinto's lead rope.

With a startled squeal, the gelding sprang forward, forced to one side by a hard jerk on his reins. Just as he did, an angry whine whipped past his ear. An instant later the crack of a rifle followed it.

The gelding was in full flight in three jumps, with Cotton hugging his neck. Two more shots smacked flatly in the still air without finding their mark.

Abruptly Cotton jerked the reins the other way, forcing the gelding into a sudden reversal, veering back to his right.

Three jumps later, the reins forced a reversal of direction again.

Twice more Cotton forced the animal to make zigzagging changes of direction at full speed. In a leftward veer, at the exact moment his pattern would have swerved him back again, he shifted his course farther left instead.

The tactic was timed perfectly. The lead projectile hurtling toward the spot where his previous pattern would have placed him passed harmlessly through empty air.

He was past the gentler slope of the approach to the river. The edge of the cliff loomed ahead. Without slackening his speed, he guided the gelding close to the edge. Gripping his rifle in his hand, he dove from the saddle. He tucked his shoulder and rolled as he hit the ground. The momentum of his dive carried him, skidding and rolling, over the lip of the cliff.

It wasn't a sheer drop-off. Not rocky enough for the sheer cliffs of the mountains, which might drop hundreds of feet, it was, nevertheless, too steep for horses or cattle.

Cotton skidded, slid and rolled thirty yards down the steep embankment before he collided with a plum bush substantial enough to arrest his descent.

He slid swiftly to the downhill side of it, keeping it between himself and the direction of the shots that had been directed at him. He sucked in great gulps of air, fighting to recover his wind and regain control of his faculties.

He pulled his rifle down where he could check the end of the barrel. He might easily have jammed it into the ground as he tumbled and slid. It was clear.

Cotton sized up the lie of the ground he could see, peering through and around the bush. Just below and in front of him, a row of cedars gripped the ground tenaciously. Their roots kept the ground beneath them from sliding downward as quickly as that in either direction. To their left, at the end of the reach of those roots, the ground fell away abruptly six or eight feet, then flattened for a few yards.

Hugging the ground, Cotton slid forward, then lowered himself into the cover the steeply eroded face of the cliff afforded him. When he reached the flatter ground, he hugged against the cliff and ran forward as far as the cover allowed. There he climbed slowly and silently.

He found the spot he wanted almost immediately. Lying on his stomach at the base of a scrub cedar, he had a clear view of the steep slope for a hundred yards. He waited there without moving.

He did not have long to wait. His hidden assailant came into view in less than ten minutes. Moving swiftly and with surprising silence, he sidled forward, rifle at the ready, eyes searching every spot of cover for his elusive quarry.

When he was well into the open, Cotton spoke softly. 'Drop the rifle!'

The man's reaction was impossibly swift. He whirled toward Cotton's voice, his rifle barking at the direction from which it came even before his head had swivelled that far. The bullet smacked into the trunk of the cedar inches above Cotton. The man had no opportunity for a second shot.

The rifle in Cotton's hand barked in response. The unmistakable thwack of lead into flesh confirmed the accuracy of his aim. The sniper grunted as he was slammed backward onto the ground. His own rifle, released from suddenly limp fingers, slid several feet down the slope before it stopped.

Silence descended on the hillside. Cotton took a deep, ragged breath. He realized for the first time that he had lost his hat. 'Better'n losin' my hide,' he thought silently.

He gathered himself to climb the hill to the dead gunman. Just as he started to move, a voice surprised him. Coming from somewhere above and to his left, a soft voice probed the cliff-side. 'You get 'im, Les? Sounded like you hit 'im, that last shot.'

Without even thinking, Cotton called back, in a normal voice, as if there were no longer any need for stealth. 'Yeah. Here.'

'Can't believe it took you that many shots to get 'im,' the voice chided. Cotton growled something he hoped would sound enough like the dead gunman, and waited.

Less than two minutes later, a second man appeared, slipping and sliding his way along the steep terrain. 'Where y'at, Les?' he questioned.

Just as Cotton opened his mouth to call out, the man spotted the dead gunman sprawled on the ground. He spit out an epithet as his gun leaped into his hand. He spotted Cotton at almost the same instant.

A split second can be a fatal amount of time. He was that much too slow in bringing his gun to bear on the unexpected presence of their intended quarry. The slug from Cotton's rifle drove the life from him instantly.

'Must've had both sides of that approach covered,' he muttered. 'I wonder if they got all the other spots watched too.'

If he moved quickly enough, it shouldn't matter. If there were others, and if they heard and investigated the burst of gunfire, he ought to be beyond the Dismal before they found the ones who had failed in their quest for his blood.

If he could recover his horses quickly enough. That and half a dozen other 'ifs' flitted through his mind. He brushed them aside, and scrambled up the face of the cliff.

17

'There ain't no way he's makin' it back here.'

Hank Houston's eyebrows were lifted in silent questioning of the statement. With the smallest flash of fear in his eyes, he ventured to respond. 'I don't know, Matt. That guy's plumb uncanny. There ain't no way a human being could survive that fire I set. It had him trapped in a spot a prairie dog couldn't have survived, clear in the bottom of his burrow, even. That thing woulda sucked him outa there an' burnt 'im to a cinder in a second. And a greyhound couldn't have outrun it. It was so big and fast and fierce I couldn't do nothin' but stand and gawk at it after it got goin'. I pertneart wet my pants knowin' I'd started that thing an' turned it loose on the range. It was like I'd called up the devil hisself an' he brung all hell with 'im, an there wasn't nothin' gonna stop it till it'd burnt up the whole country. I've thought it over an' over. There just ain't no way he coulda survived it. But he did.'

'Everybody gets lucky once in a while.'

'It ain't just luck, I'm tellin ya. He ain't human.'

'Are you tellin' me you're scared o' Lang?'

The sudden silence provided a deafening answer. Houston swallowed several times. 'Put it this way, Matt. I'd let folks call me yella afore I'd face him.'

'Then you are yellow.'

'I ain't noticed you callin' 'im out, one on one.'

Matt Dugger's face reddened. 'I'll take care of him when the time comes.'

'You figger he'll make it back here?'

'He'll try. He ain't gonna make it.'

'You're uncommon cheerful. An' certain. How can you be so sure?'

Matt studied the Texan a long

moment, too smug in his certainty not to confide in him. He just couldn't resist the opportunity to share the genius of his plan. He was almost euphoric. 'I got fourteen men watchin' for him, from every direction I can figger out he might try to sneak back. I put a price of a thousand dollars to the man that gets 'im, an' brings me his head. That scar that runs clear down across his face'll keep 'em from tryin' to bring me the wrong head. There ain't two men in the country with a scar like that. It'll cost me a thousand dollars for the guy that gets 'im, but the others won't cost me a cent.'

'Wouldn't cost you the thousand if you don't have to pay up.'

'Whatd'ya mean?'

'I mean when one of 'em gets 'im, an' brings in 'is head, I'd just take care o' that fella for half what you'd have to pay him.'

Matt snorted. 'Since when do I need you to take care o' things for me? If I do it myself, it won't cost me nothin' but the cost o' one bullet.'

Houston shrugged his shoulders to mask his disappointment. He shifted the subject. 'Are you sure you got every way covered he can come back?'

Dugger shrugged off the question as if it were a pesky fly. 'I even figgered out how that Texas drover managed to slip back, and I got two men coverin' that. If he tries to swing east an' ride the train into town thataway, his body'll end up lyin' alongside the tracks long before he gets to Ogallala. There ain't but six or eight other ways he can come, an' they're all covered.'

Houston's eyes glittered. 'Well, I ain't wishin' you no bad luck or nothin', but I'm hopin' he slips through. I wanta take care o' him myself.'

Dugger smiled broadly. Houston couldn't remember the surly rancher ever being so jolly, or so talkative. 'Are you tellin' me you're gonna face 'im?'

Houston's face reddened, but he didn't flinch. 'Oh, I'll face 'im all right, but he ain't never gonna see me. I ain't takin' no chances with that one. I'll put a slug between his eyes before he even knows I'm around.'

'Fair enough. If he makes it all the way back, he's all yours.'

'And the thousand dollars?'

'And the thousand dollars. Now go get a haircut and a shave, and get you some good clothes.'

'What? What for?'

'So you can come to my wedding.'

Houston's jaw dropped. 'Wedding! Are you gettin' married?'

Dugger's eyes glittered with a strange light Houston had never seen before. Something in it sent chills up his spine. 'Of course I'm gettin' married. I been tellin' you that all along. I've had my mind set on marryin' Esther for a long time. Tomorrow's the day.'

'She agreed to marry you?'

Dugger's wide grin dismissed any shadow of doubts that should have been there. 'She ain't gonna have no choice. I got her old man convinced she's gotta go ahead an' marry me, so she'll quit pinin' away after that Texas drifter. Among other reasons for him to agree, that is. I got the preacher to agree to be out at the Double O Bar tomorrow mornin'. Once he says the words an' signs the paper, she's all mine. Then by jing I'll put a sudden halt to her bein' so uppity. One night's all it's gonna take me to have her beggin' for more an' forgettin' all about that drifter.'

Houston's brow was furrowed with deep creases. 'But, don't she gotta agree? I mean, don't the Sky Pilot gotta ask 'er if she's willin' to be your wife?'

Dugger's eyes bored into the gunman. His voice carried a smooth assurance as unnatural as the glint in his eyes. 'Of course she does. But as her husband, I can say it for 'er, if she's slow to agree.'

Houston's frown deepened. 'But what if she tells the preacher, 'No'?'

Again, Dugger responded with absolute certainty. 'She won't.'

He didn't offer to explain the assurance, and Houston thought it best not to press the subject. He struggled through the night with the conviction that the rancher had lost his sanity. 'Acts plumb unhinged,' he was still muttering as he drifted into an uneasy sleep. He was still pondering it as they rode out of town the following morning.

Dugger and Houston both looked surprisingly good as they rode into the Double O Bar ranch yard an hour after sunup. Both were clean-shaven. Their hair was cut. Each wore a broadcloth suit. Even their boots showed at least an earnest effort with bootblack.

Both Ike and Miranda Owens were obviously dressed for a festive occasion as well. Except for their demeanor, the clothes might have been convincing. Ike, however, wore a worried frown. Miranda looked confused and angry, near the breaking-point.

'How dare you put us in a position like this,' Miranda fired at him as the pair stepped onto the porch.

'Now, Mandy, don't rile 'em,' Ike pleaded softly.

Miranda ignored him. 'Just how do you think you can ever get away with something like this?' she demanded of Dugger. 'There is nothing in the world you can threaten my daughter with that will make her accede to your demands. She would rather die than be married to the likes of you.'

Dugger's eyes glittered harshly. His voice sounded eerily like the dry rustling of a diamondback's rattle. Even so, he smiled broadly, as if enjoying something immensely funny that nobody else knew. 'An' would you rather see 'er turned over to my boys while she's still grievin' the death o' both o' you?'

Miranda's mouth opened and closed several times soundlessly. Then her power of speech returned with a rush. 'Is that what you threatened my husband with? Is that why he has agreed to this grotesque and obscene charade? What in the world makes you think you could ever, possibly, get away with such an atrocity in a civilized country? How long do you think it would take for you to be hung from the tallest cotton-wood in the country, and your body left dangling there until even the crows wouldn't touch it? And do you think for a minute — '

Her incensed tirade was cut short by the back of Dugger's hand smashing into her face. She was knocked a step backward, shocked and stunned to silence. Her hand whipped up to her face. She wiped it across her mouth, then stared wonderingly at the smear of blood across it.

Ike sprang forward to his wife's defense, but was stopped short by the muzzle of Houston's gun against his chest. Hank grinned maliciously at the rancher. 'Don't even think about it,' he warned.

Ike stopped, teetering forward on his toes in his haste to stop. He looked daggers at Dugger, but somehow held himself in check.

Dugger pushed his face inches away from Miranda's. The uncharacteristic smile was gone from his face, but his eyes continued to glimmer with a wild light. 'Listen to me, woman, an' listen good. One more outburst like that outa you, an' your ol' man's dead meat. An' you right behind 'im. An' then I'll turn that purty little gal o' yours over to my boys an' see how long she can satisfy all of 'em afore she dies from all that pleasure. That preacher's gonna be here right shortly, an' you're gonna keep your mouth shut till all's said an' done. Do you hear me?'

Miranda returned his glare with no hint of fear in her eyes. 'How do you think you can ever get a man of God to go along with something as outrageous as this? He will never pronounce a marriage in a situation like this.'

Dugger stepped back and grinned broadly again. 'If he don't, he'll die right along with the two o' you. An' it'll be you that's responsible for his death.'

'You wouldn't dare kill a man of God!' Miranda breathed.

'You try me!' Dugger challenged, as if daring a friend to a friendly wager.

'You have lost your mind!'

The smile disappeared instantly. His face contorted with a sudden rage that appalled her, even in her anger. 'That's enough, woman! One more word outa you, an' your ol' man's gonna eat lead.'

Miranda's eyes darted to Ike, still standing with Houston's gun barrel against his chest. The gunman grinned wickedly at her. 'I'm just waitin' for the word,' he assured her.

As if wiped away by some invisible hand, the rage cleared from Dugger's face, to be replaced with the affable smile. 'Where's Esther?' he demanded, his voice as casual as if he were asking for a drink of water.

Miranda's eyes involuntarily darted to the stairway leading upstairs before she caught herself and looked away. It was enough. Dugger headed for the stairs.

At the top of the steps he whipped open two bedroom doors before he got the right one. Esther was just getting dressed. As he opened that door, she gasped, jerking her dress up in front of her. 'You! What are you doing here?' she demanded.

He grinned at her, looking her up and down with open relish. 'Just waitin' for you, sweetheart,' he said. 'Get your glad rags on. You'n me's gettin' married.'

She gasped again. 'What? What on earth are you talking about? I wouldn't marry you if you were the last man on the face of the earth!'

'I ain't, but you will,' he assured her, his smile broadening even further. 'Today, as a matter o' fact. Wanta know why?'

'I don't want to know anything from you! There is no reason in the world I would ever marry you.'

'There's two reasons,' he corrected her. 'They're both downstairs. One's named Ike. The other's named Miranda. They understand real good that if you don't marry me today, they're both gonna die eatin' hot lead. There's gonna be a preacher here directly. When he gets here, you're gonna stand up with me, an' he's gonna marry us. An' if you say one word to cross things up, your pa's gonna die, your ma's gonna die, the preacher's gonna die, an' then you're gonna give yourself to me just the same as if we'da gone ahead and got married proper. Only then it'll be with you knowin' the whole time that it was really you that killed 'em all.'

Esther stared at him in wide-eyed disbelief. 'How on earth can you possibly think you could ever get away with something like that? That's insane! And if I did marry you, what then? How long do you think it would take this country to be up in arms? Why, they'd hunt you to the very ends of the earth!'

He didn't even hear the last of what she said. At the word 'insane' the smile on his face was replaced with the blind rage. His eyes glittered with an unnatural light. 'Once we're married, honey, you'll change your tune. Once you've had a real man, you'll be beggin' for more an' you won't never want nothin' or nobody in the world but me.'

As if touched by a totally different thought, his face relaxed. His broad smile returned. He continued as if his sentence hadn't been interrupted. 'An' once your folks see how happy you are, they'll know they done the right thing. Oh, they might be a mite sore for a while, but they'll come around. You'll see.'

She continued to stare uncomprehendingly at him for a long moment. 'You've completely lost your mind,' she breathed, fear and awe creeping into her voice.

The feverish glare with which he returned her stare confirmed the accuracy of her diagnosis. His instant rage was palpable. 'Think whatever you want,' he hissed, 'but keep what you're thinkin' to yourself. No wife of mine's gonna be sayin' that kinda stuff against me. The next time it happens, I'll teach you a lesson you won't never forget. Now, that preacher's gonna be here any minute, an' you an' me's gonna get hitched. So get dressed. If you ain't downstairs in ten minutes I'll come back up an' dress you myself.'

Her eyes widened even further. As if controlled by some invisible, disconnected force, his jubilant, almost bubbly grin returned. His voice assumed an air of intimate jocularity. 'An' I just might have to take off whatever you started with so's we can start from scratch. After while, that is. It might take us a while to get to the dressin' part.'

Satisfied with the incredulous gasp his words elicited, he wheeled and left the room, shutting the door behind him.

Still in a state of dazed disbelief, she arrived in the front room at almost the exact time as the preacher.

Dugger's voice was slightly loud. He continued to be uncharacteristically affable. 'You're right on time, Reverend,' he greeted him. 'We're in a mite of a hurry here, so if you could get right to it, that'd be just fine.'

He grabbed Esther's arm. Fingers digging painfully into her upper arm, he pulled her over beside himself. Esther's eyes darted to her mother, then to her father, then to Houston. In response, Houston pointedly brushed his hand across the butt of his now-holstered gun.

The preacher looked surprised and perplexed. 'My, this is most unusual. Is there a reason for the unseemly rush?'

'There's several things involved, Reverend,' Dugger evaded. 'We do need to hurry things up, though, if you don't mind.'

The preacher looked to Miranda and Ike, seeking some kind of confirmation. With a panicked glance at Esther, Ike simply nodded his assent.

After another long moment of hesitation, the preacher said, 'Very well, then, but this is highly irregular.'

He pulled a small, black book from the inside pocket of his suit coat and began to intone the words of marriage: 'Marriage is a divine appointment instituted by our beneficent Creator in the Garden of Eden when, looking upon man in his loneliness, he said: 'It is not good that the man should dwell alone . . . ' '

When he reached the part in which he asked Esther, 'Do you, Esther Owens, take this man, Matthew Dugger, to be your lawfully wedded husband?' Esther hesitated. She shot another glance at her parents, then at Houston. Her voice squeaking with a combination of fear and anger, eventually managed to mumble a barely audible, 'I do.'

The minister frowned at her hesitance. He looked at each of those in attendance again, but then, almost visibly shrugging, continued.

And then it was done. 'I now pronounce you husband and wife. You may kiss your bride.'

Dugger turned toward Esther. The fire in her eyes almost restored a moment of sanity to him. 'That'll wait till later,' he mumbled.

Already, in his fevered mind, he

pondered whether to whisk her upstairs to consummate their union immediately, or leave Houston here to guard her parents while he took her to his own place. It was hard to make a decision of such great moment while his head hurt so much. And what should he do with the preacher? What if he didn't want to leave right away?

Maybe he should just take Esther upstairs to her own room and have Hank kill them all while he was consummating his marriage.

Better yet, maybe he should make them watch. Marriages were supposed to be witnessed, weren't they? There'd be time enough to kill them all after he was finished.

There were too many options. He just couldn't think which one would be best. He'd take just a minute to think it through. Then he'd know. Then he'd act. Then Esther would be his forever.

18

'C'mon, sweetheart. We're leavin'.'

Dugger grasped his new bride roughly by the upper arm. His fingers dug into the already bruised flesh.

Esther shot a panicked, pleading look to her parents. As one, their eyes darted to Hank Houston, still standing against the wall. His hand rested idly on his gun butt. The preacher simply stared in obvious confusion.

'Where's the buggy?' Dugger demanded.

Her voice brittle with white-hot anger, Esther responded, 'I presume it is at your home.'

'Didn't I bring it?'

'That appears to be your saddle horse. I find it unlikely you carried your buggy while you rode your saddle horse.'

His face flushed dangerously. 'Don't get smart-mouthed with me, woman.'

'I would not presume to attempt to utter anything to you that might be interpreted as smart.'

His brow furrowed with thought, as if unable to decide if that were an apology or an insult. In the end he ignored it. He said, 'Where's your horse? We'll get it saddled.'

When she failed to answer, he hauled her toward the barn. She barely managed to keep her feet, stumbling in off-balance strides.

He released her in the barn, whipping her saddle from its resting place. She pondered the idea of fleeing, trying to run, to get away, to foil his crazed actions in any way she could. As soon as the idea flashed into her mind, she dismissed it. Dressed as she was, he could catch her in half a dozen strides. There was no telling what he would do then. She cast about in her mind feverishly for an alternative.

He saddled and bridled her horse with amazing speed and dexterity. Leading the horse, he grabbed her by the arm again, propelling her and her mount out into the yard.

'Get on,' he ordered.

Her eyes darted around the yard. Nothing stirred. She wondered with some part of her mind where all her father's hands were. Somebody should have been in the yard somewhere.

She thought of her parents, still held at gunpoint in the house. They would be no help. There seemed to be no alternative.

Maybe, somewhere between here and Dugger's place, she could find an opportunity to flee from him. Her horse was fast. She should be able to outrun him. She could flee all the way to Ogallala. She could ride, screaming, down the main street, summoning help.

'Get on,' he ordered again.

'Hand me the reins.' She held out her hand for them.

He laughed, one short bark. 'An' have you make a run for it? Not a chance, sweetheart. The reins is in my hands, from now on. In more ways than one.'

Her heart sank into her feet, rooting them to the spot. There had to be a way out of this predicament. She would gladly die before she would submit herself to him. But then her parents would die as well.

'The lady don't seem too anxious.'

She and Dugger whirled toward the unexpected voice. A gasp of relief and joy rushed between her lips. Dugger only growled something inarticulate, sounding more like an angry dog than a man.

Standing twenty feet away, Cotton Lang eyed Dugger carefully. His stance was casual, as if he had just stopped to pass the time of day. His hand, however, hung just at the palm-polished walnut grips of his gun.

'How'd you get here?' Dugger growled. 'You're dead.'

Cotton grinned, as if casually chatting. 'I don't look too dead, do I?'

'How'd you get here?' Dugger repeated.

'Oh, I had to take care of some of

those fellows you had staked out to make sure I didn't,' Cotton offered. 'You didn't think you could hire enough men to keep me away from Esther, did you?'

As soon as she had spotted him, Esther had begun to back away, easing silently, putting as much distance as she could between her and Dugger. As Cotton mentioned her name, Dugger's eyes darted to her. She froze in her tracks.

Dugger looked back at Cotton. 'You got no business with her,' Dugger asserted. 'This here's my wife. We been married, right an' proper.'

To say a stunned look crossed Cotton's face would be a gross understatement. He turned white, then red. He shot a look at Esther. 'What's he sayin'?' he demanded of her.

Words were caught in her throat. She couldn't free them. She opened her mouth twice, but no sound emerged. Then the dam of fear and reticence burst. A rushing torrent of words gushed from her mouth. 'Oh, Cotton, I am so happy to see you. He made me marry him. Just now, in the house. He and that Hank Houston showed up. They took Father's gun away from him. He had already arranged to have the preacher here today. He told me if I caused any trouble, or didn't agree to marry him, that Hank would kill both of my parents and the preacher too. He's lost his mind, Cotton. I said the words, but I didn't mean any of them. I just couldn't think of anything else to do. Now he's trying to take me to his place to force me to . . . to . . . Oh, Cotton, I'm so glad you've come, and now . . .'

The gush of her words might have gone on, unabated, but Dugger used the distraction to make his move. His hand whipped up from his holster with astounding speed, gripping the instrument of his rival's death.

Cotton's hand was quicker. Far quicker. Dugger's pistol hadn't lifted more than an inch above the leather of his holster when Cotton's gun barked its deterrence of Dugger's intention.

Dugger grunted, but neither moved nor halted the drawing of his weapon.

His gun was halfway between its holster and a firing position when Cotton's gun barked a second time.

That time, Dugger made no sound. His gun continued the arc of its ascent to deadly elevation. It leveled as Cotton's gun barked a third time. Each time he fired, Cotton took a short step to one side. As Dugger's gun leveled, it roared fire and death toward his nemesis. The bullet tore through Cotton's shirt, just below his left arm.

As he felt the tug of the bullet's near miss, Cotton lifted the barrel of his gun slightly. The fourth slug from his gun slammed through the bridge of Dugger's nose, exiting through the back of his head. He flopped backward on the ground instantly. His gun flew from suddenly slack fingers, even as he toppled.

Cotton shook his head in disbelief,

staring at the supine body of his antagonist. 'How can a man stand there like a rock an' take three slugs in the heart and keep standing?' he marveled.

Then Esther was in his arms, her own arms wrapped as tightly as bands of steel around him. Her head was buried in his shoulder. 'Oh, Cotton, my darling, I don't know how you got here, or anything you've been through, but I have never been so glad to see anyone in my life. I'm never, ever, going to let you out of my sight again, for as long as I live. Oh, Cotton! It was so awful. So terrible. I was so terrified. I didn't have any idea what I could do. He was so crazy. He would be this absolutely wild, crazed madman one minute, threatening things I don't even want to think about. Then he would change, like something totally different came over him, and he would smile and laugh and make jokes about how he was going to . . . Oh, Cotton, I don't know what I would have done — '

Once again the rushing tide of words

was stemmed abruptly. A shotgun roared from the porch of the house.

Cotton thrust Esther away so forcefully she sprawled on the ground. His gun swung toward the sound. 'Only one shot left,' his mind warned him. 'Took four bullets just for Dugger.'

His instant of panic was replaced by a flood of relief. Just as his eyes found him, Hank Houston crashed to the ground. Puffs of dust erupted from around him as he landed.

On the porch of the house, Ike Owens held a double-barreled shotgun at waist level, pointing at the spot where Dugger's enforcer had stood seconds before. His face was twisted in unspeakable anger. His mouth was working, silently speaking words he couldn't put voice to. He walked toward the supine gunman. The shotgun roared again, and Houston's body jerked with the impact.

Ike pulled both hammers back. He continued to advance, again squeezing the triggers, one at a time.

Instead of a shotgun's roar, each pull

of the trigger was followed only by the click of the hammer onto an already spent shell. He seemed not to notice.

He continued to advance, cocking and firing the empty weapon half a dozen times. The last time, he held the end of the barrels right against the dead man's forehead and pulled both triggers at once.

Miranda Owens, flying from the porch, grabbed her husband. Trying to haul him away from the object of his wrath, she pleaded, 'Ike! Ike! It's OK, honey. It's all right now. He's dead, Ike. Ike, your gun's empty. It's all over, Ike.'

Ike turned his head and looked into his wife's face. He blinked several times. He raised his head and looked around the yard. His eyes rested briefly on Dugger's body, then on Cotton, then came to bear on Esther. He blinked several more times. The shotgun slipped from his fingers, falling onto the man it had dispatched.

Esther broke into a run, arms outstretched toward her father. 'Oh,

Father, Father, you're all right. Father, Cotton made it back. He killed Dugger.'

She ran into her father's out-stretched arms and was lost in an embrace of relief and joy. Miranda, seemingly the calmest person in the yard, spoke to Cotton. 'Hank was going to shoot you in the back,' she said. 'He had taken Ike's gun away from him, but he didn't know Ike always keeps a shotgun behind the front door. As soon as he went outside to kill you, Ike grabbed it and shot him before he could shoot you. I'm so glad you're back, Cotton.'

With the resilience of a man who had carved a ranch out of hostile country, Ike spoke. His voice was normal, comically casual. 'I don't suppose you could've got here just a mite sooner?' he questioned. 'You was cuttin' things plumb awful close.'

Laughing with near incoherence, Esther rushed back to Cotton. This time he was ready for her. Preventing what might have been another rushing tide of words, his lips closed against hers.

After a long moment, she backed her head away slightly. A jaunty air abruptly replaced her air of frantic relief. 'Hey, cowboy,' she offered with exaggerated flippancy, 'we just happen to have a preacher up at the house. You wouldn't by chance be interested in gettin' hitched, would you?'

He let his actions answer the question she didn't really need to ask.

We do hope that you have enjoyed reading this large print book.

Did you know that all of our titles are available for purchase?

We publish a wide range of high quality large print books including:
Romances, Mysteries, Classics
General Fiction
Non Fiction and Westerns

Special interest titles available in large print are:
The Little Oxford Dictionary
Music Book, Song Book
Hymn Book, Service Book

Also available from us courtesy of Oxford University Press:
Young Readers' Dictionary
(large print edition)
Young Readers' Thesaurus
(large print edition)

For further information or a free brochure, please contact us at:
Ulverscroft Large Print Books Ltd.,
The Green, Bradgate Road, Anstey,
Leicester, LE7 7FU, England.
Tel: (00 44) **0116 236 4325**
Fax: (00 44) **0116 234 0205**

LAST MILE TO NOGALES

Ryan Bodie

Nogales was a hell town, in the heart of the desert. Its single claim to fame was its band of deadly guns-for-hire who lived there, especially Ryan Coder, whom some saw as the gun king. Yet Coder found his life on the line when he hired out to the king of Chad Valley and was pitted against Holly, the youngest and deadliest gunslinger of them all. Would Coder end up just another notch on Holly's gun?

THE DEVIL'S RIDER

Lance Howard

When vicious outlaw Jeremy Trask escapes the hangman's noose, he rides into Baton Ridge on a mission of revenge and bloodlust. It had been a year since he'd murdered manhunter Jim Darrow's brother in cold blood. Now, along with the sole survivor of the massacre, a young homeless widow named Spring Trel-ler, Darrow vows to hunt down the outlaw — this time to finish him for good. But will he survive the deadly reception the outlaw has waiting?